Idol

Thoughts

Book One
in the
H3RO Series

An Atlantis Entertainment Novel

J. S. Lee

Axellia Publishing

CONTENTS

DEDICATION

This book is dedicated to Cheryl. Without her, I wouldn't have been able to write this book—literally.

Thank you, Cheryl, for your license gift for Microsoft Word!

THE ATLANTIS ENTERTAINMENT UNIVERSE

Reverse Harem
(As J. S. Lee)

H3RO

Idol Thoughts
Idol Worship
Idol Gossip

Onyx

ONYX: Truth
ONYX: Heart
ONYX: Love
ONYX: Unity
ONYX: Forever

Young Adult Contemporary Romance
(As Ji Soo Lee)

Zodiac

The Idol Who Became Her World
The Girl Who Gave Him The Moon
The Dancer Who Saved Her Soul
The Leader Who Fell From The Sky

—

K-101

For those of you unfamiliar with K-Pop / K-Dramas / Korean culture, here's a short handy guide:

Names

Names in Korean are written family name then given name. It's not uncommon to use the full name when addressing a person—even one you're close to.

박현태 is the Korean way of writing Park Hyuntae (Tae). Tae is pronounced like Tay.

권민혁 is the Korean way of writing Kwon Minhyuk

하균구 is the Korean way of writing Ha Kyungu (Kyun)

송준기 is the Korean way of writing Song Junki (Jun)

Nate and Dante are a little different as they are American-Korean and Chinese. Nate isn't a Korean name and would therefore be spelled out phonetically in Korean. The same for Dante. (For those curious, it would be 네이트 for Nate, and 단테 for Dante.)

Surnames (Family names)

As the western worlds combined, we ended up with a lot of variation in surnames. In Korea, although there is variation, you will find a lot Kims, Lees, and Parks. To try to keep things as easy to follow as possible, I have tried to make sure that all characters don't have the same surname *unless* they're in the same family—like Holly. However, in reality, this is most often not the case.

BTS, for example have Kim Namjoon (RM), Kim Seokjin (Jin), and Kim Taehyung (V). They all share the same family name, but are not related.

Oppa (오빠), hyung (형), noona (누나), and oennie (언니)

This one gets a little confusing at first. The first thing you need to know, in Korea, age is a very important thing. It's not uncommon for you to be asked your age before your name because you need to be spoken to with the correct level of respect (known as honorifics). To show this, there's actually several ways to speak to address a person and it usually depends on your age (an exception to this might be in a place of work where someone younger than you is more senior to you). But I'll keep this simple and limit myself to terms used in the book.

Traditionally, oppa, hyung, noona, and unnie are terms used to describe your older sibling—depending on what sex you are and what sex they are. If you are male, your older brother is hyung and your older sister is noona. If you are female, your older brother is your oppa, and your older sister is unnie (technically, 언니 when Romanized is oenni, but unnie has become a more standard way of writing this). However, this can often be transferred to people you are close to. A girl will call her older boyfriend oppa. An idol will call his older groupmates hyung.

Sunbae (선배) and Hoobae (후배)

Along the same vein, sunbae (senior) and hoobae (junior) may be used as an alternative when using experience as a basis, rather than age.

Other

Comeback: this is an odd one for most people. Your next single isn't just your next single. It's a comeback—and it doesn't matter if you've waited two months or two years.

Kakao: Kakao is a messaging app similar to Whatsapp or Wechat.

SNS: What we would call Social Media, Koreans use the term Social Networking Service. Included in this would be **V Live**, an app which allows Korean idols to communicate with their fans (a bit like Instagram Live)

화이팅: Fighting, or 'hwaiting' is a word commonly used as encouragement, like 'good luck' or 'let's do this'.

Maknae: a term used for the youngest member of a group.

'Ya!': The Korean equivalent to 'Hey!'

제 X 장: Chapter (pronounced jae X jang)

Character Bios are also available at the back of this book

More terms and information are available on Ji Soo's website:
www.jislooleeauthor.com/k101

제1 장

H3RO

Hero

"H3RO is a problem group."

"True, and they are one of the worst earners in Atlantis," another agreed.

"Financially, they are worth more separate than together," a third threw his argument into the ring. "But they have nearly a year left on their contracts. It would cost us more to end their contracts now."

I sat in silence, trying to follow the argument. It was hard work when my Korean was rusty, and I had no idea about anything in the music industry. Only six months ago, my mom announced that my father was Lee Woojin, Chairman of Atlantis Entertainment—one of the top five powerhouse K-Pop entertainment companies in South Korea. I'd grown up in Chicago with my mom, knowing only that my dad was in Korea and his family had never approved of her.

Lee Woojin (I was not calling him Dad), had contacted my mom out of the blue to say he wanted me back in Seoul because it was time that I joined the family business. What the hell did I know about the music industry?

Jack shit. I had just graduated college with a Masters in English Literature and had been helping my mom out in her restaurant while trying to find a full-time job. At no point in my educational career (or at any point in the twenty-four years of my life, for that matter), had I considered the music industry.

My mom had insisted I go: she wanted me to get to know my father, especially as we hadn't heard from him since she had left Korea. Woojin just wanted me back, regardless of my opinion. Two months later, I had moved; under the agreement that I would stay in my own place. I was not prepared to move in with him.

After a two-month grace period, I had gotten settled in Seoul, trying to revive the Korean my mom had taught me growing up but I had gotten out of the habit of speaking while being at college. Then I had been thrown into the corporate world of Atlantis Entertainment, where the only women seemed to be the receptionists, the makeup artists, and the idols themselves. It was a very male dominated company where no one wanted to teach me anything but expected me to know everything.

Which was why I sat clueless in this meeting, listening to five men argue with my half-brother (by blood only), Sejin. The guy hated me, because I, the illegitimate child of the Lee family, had moved in on the company he was set to take over. A company where nobody other than Woojin and Sejin knew who I was. My relationship was to be kept hidden.

For now, at least.

Despite the secrecy, Sejin hated me. If he spent five minutes with me, he would realize very quickly that was the *last* thing I wanted.

From what I could follow, they were discussing the various artists and groups on their roster, trying to work out which were making money, and which were costing Atlantis Entertainment. Apart from a couple of names mentioned, I really didn't know who was who.

"… Holly? Or do you think you're too good for that challenge?"

I blinked at the sound of my name, realizing Sejin was talking to me—in English. I gave him a pleasant smile. "Of course," I responded, positively. I had no idea what he had put me forward for, and a large part of me was sure it was something I was designed to fail, but anything would be better than this.

"Then it is settled. Holly will move in with them this evening. We will have schedules sent to you this afternoon."

I blinked again. Move in where? Internally I was panicking, but I kept my expression as calm as possible. I was not going to let Sejin know he had unsettled me. I managed to keep the serenity for the rest of the meeting. It wasn't until I was in my own office, staring out at the incredible view of the Han River, that I allowed myself to freak out. What the hell had I agreed to?

There was a knock at the door and a guy who looked vaguely familiar stepped in carrying a folder. He didn't look happy. "Hello," I greeted him.

"Hello," he returned. "I am Shin Hanjoo. I am H3RO's manager—former manager."

I stared blankly at him. "How can I help you?"

"What do you know about managing a group?"

I shrugged. "Nothing."

Hanjoo muttered something under his breath that I didn't catch, before thrusting the folder at me. "I don't know where you came from, or how you've suddenly become their manager, but I have been with these boys for eight years; long before they debuted. I beg of you, please look after them."

Before I could ask him what he was talking about, he looked panicked and darted from the room. With a frown, I looked at the folder, quickly skimming through it. In it were all the bios of a group. "Oh, hell no," I muttered.

I tossed the folder onto the desk and left my office, marching down to Sejin's. I pushed the door open, not caring if he was alone or not. Forget etiquette. "Did you fire a perfectly good manager to replace him with me?" I demanded.

Sejin looked up from his computer and smiled. "Do come in, Holly."

I strode in, slamming the door behind me. "Did you?"

"Over the last six years, H3RO have developed a reputation for being late and unreliable. Ha Kyungu has had no end of promotional absences. Nate Choi will not stop making headlines for drinking, and we've had to step in to stop assault charges being filed too many times. They've also never had a number one single or album. So, in answer to your question: no, I am not firing a perfectly good manager. I am firing a terrible one."

I wasn't convinced all of that was Hanjoo's fault. But that wasn't the important part right now. "And you decided to pick me to replace him?"

The smile Sejin gave me was positively evil. "I

thought you were up to the challenge? I can tell father if that's not the case?"

Although my hands were balled into fists beside me, I forced myself to count to ten before responding. *Fuck him.* I was good at thinking on my feet. I would damn well learn. "No, I'm not backing down from this challenge," I told him.

"Good," Sejin smiled. "You will be their manager for their next comeback. I want an album out and finalized by the end of next month, to be released the following month, with no scheduling mishaps. I want H3RO to have a number one single."

"I'll get you two," I declared, regretting it as soon as the smug smirk appeared on Sejin's face. I turned on my heel and marched out of the room.

I returned to my office and sank into the large chair behind my desk. While reaching for the folder I had discarded earlier, I kicked off my shoes. Twenty minutes later, I was contemplating booking a flight back to Chicago. I forced myself to push the thought aside. I was not going to let Sejin win this easily. I read through the information I had been given, trying to take it all in.

H3RO had debuted just over six years ago, and in that time, they had never won anything. They also had nothing ready for an album which was to be finished in a little over seven weeks' time. How quickly could you put an album together?

I was beginning to suspect that the main reason this groups wasn't doing well was because of the company managing it. My half-brother was an asshole.

H3RO

During the afternoon, as promised, a schedule appeared. Well, 'schedule' was a very generous term for the piece of paper I was given. It was nearly empty. I had then tried to find someone in the company who was willing to help me. I wasn't asking for an album to be handed over to me, although I wouldn't have turned that down. What I was after was a little guidance as to what I needed to do to get there, or even where to make a start.

Not a single person would help me.

One person came close, but as soon as he opened his mouth, he closed it, before scuttling away. I glanced over my shoulder and found Sejin lingering in the background. *Asshole*. He wasn't going to make this easy for me.

I wasn't going to give up that easily though.

I had spent several hours surfing the internet, looking for the answers. By nightfall, I was tired, hungry, and once again contemplating booking that flight back to America. My alarm stopped that—I had set it to make sure I left on time every day. Now all I needed to do was get back to my apartment and pack up my things, so I could head over to the dorm H3RO shared.

Despite being in my apartment for two months, I thankfully hadn't done much in the way of unpacking. I'd gone out and bought a few new suits and dresses, but for the most part, packing was quick. I stuck it all in the back of the brand-new Range Rover Lee Woojin had provided me with when I moved over here. It was a nice drive, but no matter what, I couldn't stop myself from thinking of it as guilt money.

My apartment and the dorms were on opposite

sides of the Gangnam district of Seoul, but with the rush hour traffic long gone, it was a quick drive. I parked in the underground parking lot and found the elevator.

From what I had learned, Atlantis provided groups with something between a dorm and an apartment. A private communal area, and bedrooms. One per group. It wasn't until I was standing outside H3RO's apartment that I wondered where exactly I was supposed to stay. Surely, they wouldn't have me actually living with them? One woman in a house full of men? In Korea? I was the same age as some of them. The fans, never mind the news, would definitely not be happy with that!

And yet, I had been given a code for this door.

Just entering the code into the lock felt rude. Instead, I knocked on the door and waited. The door opened a few seconds later. "Oh, shit," I muttered, staring up at an exceptionally good-looking guy. At five feet and six inches, a lot of guys were taller than me. Even with these heels on, giving me an extra three inches, this guy towered above me still.

He tilted his head and stared down at me, an eyebrow disappearing under a mass of unbrushed waves. Park Hyuntae, Tae, was six foot something of brooding sex appeal. "That's new," he responded. "Hello to you, too." He had dark, serious eyes; too serious for someone who was only a couple of years older than me.

"Oh, shit," I muttered again. "I mean, hello." Although his expression wasn't severe, he continued to stare at me, expectantly. "I'm Holly Lee," I quickly introduced myself. "I don't know if—"

"Oh," he shrugged, stepping back to let me in. I

gave him a brief smile and stepped inside, dragging my two cases behind me.

The place was smaller than I expected. Much smaller. The main area consisted of a small open-planned living area. There were two small couches looking a little worse for wear, on top of one were two more guys focused on a console game on a small television in front of them. To my side was more of a kitchenette than a kitchen, though it had a thin island, and in between the two areas was a low table. There was a small corridor going off to one side, but judging from the size of this area, I wasn't convinced these guys had their own room.

No one really expected me to stay here, right?

While I was busy looking around, Tae had walked over to the TV. "You guys might want to pause that," he said, nodding his head at me.

One of them did so, then both turned and peered over the back of the couch at me. I sucked in a deep breath. Two more gorgeous humans. I realized that the small passport style photos I'd seen in their bios this morning did them absolutely no justice at all. They had also been taken so long ago, it hadn't occurred to me they wouldn't look anything like their headshots: young men, not boys.

I gave them an awkward finger wave. "I'm Holly."

The mouth of one on the couch fell open. "They sent a woman?"

The guy next to him smacked him upside the head. "They have female managers in the America." Ah, so that was Nate Choi. He was the only American-Korean in the group, the fact given away by him referring to America in English. If I recalled correctly, he was the same age as me: twenty-four.

If I wasn't mistaken, the guy next to him was the group's maknae, the youngest, Song Junki, JunK. The only resemblance to his pre-debut headshot was the mischievousness in his eyes. Holy hell ... talk about a glow-up!

"We're not in America," JunK pointed out. "And we're not a girl group."

"You're here to disband us, aren't you?" a voice from behind asked, making me jump.

I whirled around, forgetting I was in heels. Before I could stop myself, a foot went from under me and I could feel myself heading for the ground.

And then I wasn't.

I poked an eye open and found myself in the arms of the group's alleged troublemaker, Kyun. I stared up at him, surprised at how firm his arms felt. "Well?" he demanded, setting me upright and snapping me out of a trance.

"Thank you," I said, feeling my face heat up.

"Are you here to disband us?" Kyun asked with a scowl. If Tae was serious, Kyun looked ... angry.

I shook my head. "I'm here for you guys, to get your next album out," I told him, omitting the fact I was also here to prove a point to Sejin—and everyone else at Atlantis Entertainment.

"Sure," Kyun muttered disbelievingly. He turned, disappearing back down the corridor. I glanced back at the other three. None of them looked surprised at Kyun's behavior.

"Would you like me to show you to your room?" Tae asked.

"I am staying here?" I blurted out.

Tae nodded, "Hanjoo said to clean up the room for you."

I blew out a breath as JunK broke out into a cheeky grin. "You can always share with me, if you like?"

That earned him a punch from Nate. "What about me?"

JunK rolled his eyes. "Fine, you can sleep with me and Nate, if you want?" he corrected himself, before fixing his attention on me. He didn't break his stare as he locked eyes at me, and I could feel my face heat up once more as some inappropriate images of what sharing a room with JunK and Nate would entail.

I cleared my throat, looking to Tae. "Yes, please," I said, not missing the smirk settle on JunK's lips. Tae pointed down the small corridor. I led the way, Tae following behind with my second case.

My room was the last one at the end of the corridor. I pushed the door open and walked in. It was small: cozy. There was something about it which reminded me of home. I pulled my case in and turned, ready to take the second off Tae, but I wasn't expecting him to be standing so close behind me.

I walked straight into him, bouncing back. Although I managed to keep my balance, his hands shot out and grasped my shoulders to steady me. "Are you here to disband us?" he asked, softly, his dark eyes scanning my face.

I stared up at him. There was no denying his face was handsome. His hair was soft and fluffy with a slight wave to it, like he had let it dry naturally. It fell over his forehead, brushing his thick eyebrows. "I have no intention of doing that," I assured him. "I'm here for a comeback."

Tae's face dropped lower, his eyes staring deep into mine. His face was so close to mine, that my mouth went dry. Sad eyes and a stern face somehow made for a dangerous combination. I quickly wet my lips. His gaze dropped to watch the action, then very slowly, he was staring into my eyes again. "The bathroom is directly opposite," he finally announced before disappearing from the bedroom.

I watched him leave, pulling the door closed behind him. What had happened to this group, to Tae, to cause those sad eyes?

Even though I wasn't sure I would like the answers, I found myself wanting to uncover that mystery.

제2 장

H3R오

Boss

I unpacked a few things, hanging up the suits and dresses I had so they didn't wrinkle, and found my toothbrush. It was getting late and I was exhausted. When I left my bedroom, I could hear voices coming from the living area. I wasn't one for eavesdropping, so I hurried over to the bathroom, locking the door behind me.

I used the facilities and was lost in thought while brushing my teeth when the door rattled. Before I could spit the toothpaste out to call out and say that it was occupied, the door opened, and someone strode in.

At first, I had no idea who it was. I was too busy staring at the very naked body in front of me. This guy worked out: there was nothing but muscle. He had the most amazing shoulders I had seen for a long time, and wrapped over the top of them, curling down his back, was the tattoo of a tail, though I couldn't tell what it belonged to. He was also in possession of a very defined eight-pack, and underneath a thin trail of black hair … holy hell, he was huge!

My mouth dropped open, and my toothbrush fell out with a soft clatter on the tiled floor.

"Who are you?" he demanded.

I finally pull my eyes away, bringing them up to meet the eyes of the person staring at me. Guan Feng, from Hong Kong, usually went by his stage name, Dante. His head was tilted as he stared at me. Although he was carrying a towel, he made no attempt to cover himself up. Then my brain kicked into gear and I turned my head to the sink.

"Why is there a woman in the bathroom?" he bellowed out of the room as I spat my toothpaste out.

"Do you want to cover yourself up?" I spluttered, refusing to look in his direction.

"Do you want to explain why you're in my bathroom?"

At that moment, there was an explosion of laughter and JunK appeared behind Dante, cackling with sheer entertainment.

"The door was locked," I said, trying to explain why Dante was naked in the bathroom with me. "And why are you still naked?" I demanded. I grabbed my things and marched past them both, doing my best to avoid touching Dante (not an easy feat when he was standing in the doorway), to return to my room.

Inside, I closed the door, leaning against it. "You said the bathroom was free," I heard Dante say. There was more laughter, and then an 'ooph' from what I guessed was a punch to the gut. "Who the hell is she?"

"That's our new manager, hyung," JunK told him. I could hear him running away down the corridor laughing again. Slowly, I slid down the door. *Holy hell*, I needed a shower. A cold shower. But there was no way

I was leaving this bedroom again tonight.

H3RO

Once I had pulled a suit on and was fully clothed, I left my bedroom to use the bathroom. This time I put a hair scrunchie around the door handle, like I was back at college, and proceeded to wedge the door shut so I could wash. It was possibly too early for the others to be up, but I managed to successfully use the bathroom in peace.

I emerged to sounds of life coming from the living area. After leaving my wash things in my bedroom, but collecting my iPad, I headed down there. Busy cooking up breakfast was the final member of H3RO: Minhyuk. He was currently sporting longish hair which was tied back around the nape of his neck.

With his attention fixed on making an omelet, I didn't want to disturb him and risk startling him. Instead, I moved over to the window to check out the view. We weren't far from the Atlantis building. I could see the green glass windows just down the road from where the dorms were. At least getting to the office would be simple enough, unlike my place which was on the other side of Gangnam.

"Who are you?"

I turned and found Minhyuk staring at me, the frying pan in one hand and the chopsticks he was using instead of a spatula in the other. Of all of the members, he had the most delicate features: a thin face, pointed chin, and the palest skin.

"Good morning," I greeted him cheerfully. "I hope I didn't startle you. I'm Holly. Your new manager."

"Really?" he asked, surprised. When I nodded, he shrugged. "Have you eaten?"

I shook my head, my stomach giving a small grumble to confirm. "No."

"Take a seat," he said, nodding to the table. "It will be ready soon." I glanced at the table, wondering if there were assigned seats. "Hanjoo used to sit at the head of the table," Minhyuk offered.

I wasn't sure if taking his seat or one of the others was worse, but I sat where Minhyuk suggested. "Would you like some help?" I asked, itching for something to do.

"I'm nearly done," Minhyuk assured me. "The others will be in here soon."

Minhyuk was busy placing the side dishes on the table when the others, one by one, started to emerge. There were some surprised looks when they found me in Hanjoo's seat, but thankfully no one offered any comment.

I picked at the rice bowl, no longer feeling my appetite, despite the breakfast spread in front of me. Finally, under Kyun's scowl, I set my chopsticks down with a sigh. "To be clear, I am not here to disband you," I announced to the silent room. "My intention is to give you a comeback and a number one."

"Is that your job?" Tae asked, suspiciously.

"It's the job Lee Sejin gave me," I nodded. "I have every intention of seeing it through, provided that's what you want?" I asked. "It has been a while since your last release."

"Not because we wanted it that way," JunK told me. "We've been asking for a comeback for ages. We thought the company had forgotten us." That earned him a swipe to the shoulder from Dante.

I held my hands up. "I don't really know what has gone on before me," I said. "I'm not here to report back. Like I said, I'm here to get H3RO topping the charts."

"What do you have for us?" Tae asked.

"What do you mean?" I replied, frowning.

"What are the songs?"

"There are none," I said with a shrug. "It's your album. It's up to you guys to write them." Six pairs of eyes stared at me. "What?"

"We have always used the company's songs," Tae told me, still staring at me in astonishment.

I chewed at my lower lip, before deciding to tell the truth. "I got sent one song. It was … it wasn't good. When I complained to Sejin, he told me that the songwriters and producers were unavailable until later in the year."

"All of them?" Nate asked in disbelief.

I nodded. "What's the problem? You guys have been together six years. Longer if you include your pre-debut. Surely in that time you've written stuff yourself?"

Collectively, the group looked at each other. "Can't we just wait until the writers are ready?" Minhyuk asked, brushing the long, stray hair from his face.

I looked at the group with a frown. "We need to have the album released by the end of next month."

"That's what? Seven weeks!" Dante exclaimed as the room broke into noisy objections.

"That's plenty of time," I responded, calmly, over the commotion.

"If we had songs, maybe," JunK objected. "We

don't."

"Again, I ask if you have anything already? And if not, so what? Your schedules are empty. Let's work together and get something out there. We only need six songs."

There was a jangle as Kyun threw down his chopsticks, the metal clattering against the china, and then he stood up and stormed out of the room. The guys shared another collective look, and then Tae hurried after him. I watched them leave, my eyes wide. "What did I say?"

The four remaining members shared another look and then JunK shrugged. He turned to me. "We're no good."

"Huh?" I said, staring blankly at him.

"We haven't had a single one of our songs on any of our albums," he explained. "They've always been written for us."

"But you have written songs?" I asked, slowly.

Nate nodded. "But they're no good."

My eyes went wide again. "I don't understand."

Dante let out a sigh. "We regularly go to Sejin with our own music, but they've never been good enough."

"He said that?" I asked in disbelief.

"Well, that's the polite version," Nate muttered. "But as writers, we suck."

I licked my lips, trying to keep myself from exploding. "Excuse me," I muttered, getting up. I left the apartment, just in time before my hands started shaking. To say I was angry was an understatement. I made for the stairs and marched up six more flights to the roof. By the time I was outside, I was only marginally calmer. The roof of the dorms had a small garden. I paced back and forth, until eventually my anger won out and I pulled my phone out of my pocket.

I called Sejin. He answered on the second ring. "What do you want, Holly?"

"Have you honestly been telling H3RO for the last *six* years that they are no good at songwriting?" I demanded.

"They do not have any skills to make a half decent single," came the response. "Would you have me lie to them?"

"I would have you encourage them," I snapped at him. "If someone comes to you with an interest in something, something which you have a modicum of power over, you help them out. If they're not good, that's OK, but you've had six years to help them grow and develop."

There was an impatient sigh. "Holly, don't start arguing with me over things you know nothing about. They have no talent. It's no use wasting resources on them."

I froze. "Wasting resources?" I repeated, feeling my blood go cold.

"Yes," Sejin said, curtly. "Wasting resources on talentless individuals. It's nothing personal: it's business."

"If they had no talent, why would you ..." I trailed off. "Are all the writers really busy, or do you just consider that *wasting resources*?" I demanded.

"Holly, do you have anything to say worth listening to?"

My free hand curled back into a fist. It was a good job we were not in the same room. "You are an asshole,

Sejin. An asshole who has just met his match with his sister. Not only am I going to show you exactly what I'm made of, H3RO is going to have their most successful comeback and it will be all their own hard work." I ended the call before he could say anything and launched the phone at the floor.

I marched over to the edge of the building, Atlantis Entertainment's offices in front of me, and clutched at the wall. "Fuck you, Sejin!" I yelled.

That made me feel a little better. The energy left me, and I hung my head, shaking it in disbelief. H3RO's future was being screwed with because my half-brother hated my existence. That wasn't fair on them. I shook my head. "They are not going to fail because of me."

"Your screen is cracked, but it still seems to be working," a voice said as my phone appeared under my nose.

I let out a startled squeal and jumped backwards. "Nate!" I took the phone from him, clutching it to my chest as my heart pounded. "How much of that did you hear?"

He stared at me from under his thick, dark fringe, then shrugged, casually leaning back against the wall. "All of it."

"I swear I am not here to get you disbanded," I told him, finally. "I am going to do *everything* I can to get you guys to have a successful comeback."

"Sejin's your brother?"

I drummed my fingers against my phone and nodded. "Which means Lee Woojin, Chairman of Atlantis Entertainment is also my father. He had an affair with my Mom, and she had me in America. I found out about six months ago, when Woojin

19

demanded I move out here and learn the family business. Sejin hates me. He never bothered asking if this illegitimate child was happy with any of this." I sighed and looked away. "I'm sorry, H3RO is being used as a weapon in my family drama."

"I heard all the conversation," Nate repeated. "Or at least your side of it. I don't think you're out to do us any harm. Intentionally, at least." I glanced over at him as he scratched his head. "I think it would be for the best if we didn't mention it to the others though."

I nodded. "Thank you," I muttered.

He frowned. "Do you know anything about K-Pop? About the music industry in general?" The frown deepened. "About Korea?"

Not anywhere near enough to be working here. I just shook my head.

"At least you can speak the language," he sighed. "I had to spend months learning it. I still get it mixed up sometimes." He gave me a small smile. "You know it's not going to be easy?" he asked. "Getting us a successful comeback, especially when you don't know anything about this world?"

"Who said I'm doing it alone?" I returned. "It's your comeback. You're the ones who are going to be writing, recording, and performing. I'm just going to be your cheerleader the whole way."

제3 장

H3RO

Hey You!

I spent the day on the roof. Up there was a cabana-esque structure which offered some shelter from the sun, but also covered a couch and a pile of cushions to stretch out on. Most importantly, there was a power outlet. I had expected the warm weather to draw everyone out, but the roof remained empty.

I took advantage of it, spending my time alternating between reading company files, watching videos on YouTube, and researching on Naver, the Korean equivalent of Google. By the end of the day, I had fallen down the deep, dark rabbit hole that was K-Pop, and was wondering how I had gone so long without it in my life.

What I'd also discovered, from watching the three live shows H3RO had ever been on, was that they were talented. Regardless of whether they wrote their own music or not, they could sing or rap, they could dance, and holy hell, they were all beautiful. It was also painfully clear that they had been let down by Atlantis Entertainment.

Not anymore.

By late evening, as the sun had started to dip behind the taller buildings, and as the motion sensitive lights had kicked in, I was feeling somewhere between determined and completely lost. Atlantis had never given these guys a fair shot at anything. Even now, the budget might just cover the album distribution—or at least Sejin's low aspirations as to how many copies they would be able to sell.

I would also admit I was in way over my head. I had zero experience at this. Sejin was setting me up to fail by being as restrictive as possible and making sure there was no guidance.

I dropped my phone on the cushion beside me and allowed my head to fall into my hands. That was the eighth attempt at calling Sejin, and he was obviously ignoring my calls. I would have to go into Atlantis tomorrow and wait him out in his office if I had to. And if that didn't work, I would go one step above him and talk to Woojin. If daddy dearest wanted me to be a part of this company, he needed to make sure Sejin was playing fair.

"Are you hungry?"

I looked up and found Nate heading towards me, carrying a bowl of ramyun. My stomach grumbled appreciatively at that in answer. "Thank you," I sighed, inhaling a steamy delicious whiff of the food. The last thing I had eaten was Minhyuk's breakfast and I had abandoned half of that. Lost in a blackhole of YouTube videos and sibling rage, I had forgotten I needed to eat and drink.

A large bottle of water was placed beside the bowl. "You might want that too."

I nodded, wearily. "Thank you," I said, again. I reached for the disposable chopsticks, breaking them in two, and giving the ramyun a stir.

"Minhyuk's the best cook. I can boil water," Nate said. He took a seat beside me and pointed at the video that was paused. "That was our most successful single." 'Loved Up' was their second single. It had scraped in the bottom of the charts for a week before disappearing into oblivion.

"How is it in the dorm?" I asked in between shoveling noodles into my mouth.

Nate scratched at the back of his head, sending his hair dancing behind him. Unlike Tae's it fell naturally straight, but favored a center parting. "It's not very positive, to be honest."

"Is everyone that scared of writing their own material?"

"We're not good, and we know it," Nate shrugged, his broad shoulders pulling at his T-shirt. "None of us really want to put ourselves out there to fail."

I finished inhaling the noodles and took a long drink of water before responding to that. "Nate, your best hit—your *best* hit—got to 38 on the Gaon Digital Chart. That was the *only* chart it landed on. That was written by a professional."

"Yeah, so what makes you think we can do any better?" Nate asked, looking crestfallen.

I stared at him wanting to tell him the truth: that I'd spent the afternoon listening to every single and album H3RO had released. I then looked at who had written them. Not one of the writers were Atlantis' most successful songwriters. Not even one of them was from a mid-ranking songwriter. All of them had been written by someone who had written one song for Atlantis and then been shown the door.

I was beginning to question why H3RO had debuted to start with. I could certainly see why a room of financial experts wanted to disband them. It was costing them more to feed and board them than what they were making from them. Honestly, they were making a loss for the company.

I didn't say that. Instead, I rubbed at my neck, trying to work out a kink. Beside me, Nate got on his knees and moved behind me, removing my hand and replacing them with his. Through the thin fabric of my dress, I could feel the heat that was radiating from his hands as he massaged my neck and shoulders.

"Because you're all still here," I told him eventually. I pointed at the video. "Because, even in your last single, I could see in your eyes how much you wanted it. And because I refuse to believe that even though you've all been told you have no talent when it comes to writing, that you all just gave up."

His massage stopped. "Do you really mean that?"

I glanced up behind me to look at him and nodded. "I have a feeling I believe it more than you do."

H3RO

I was up early the following morning. Aside from wanting to take a shower before everyone else was up and avoid running the risk of someone walking in on me, I wanted to get to Atlantis before Sejin. I had to wait an hour, his secretary sending me strange looks the entire time, but I wasn't giving up that easily.

He either didn't see me or ignored me as he walked into his office. I followed him, ignoring the secretary's protests. "Stop being an asshole and taking out your frustrations on H3RO!" I declared, following him to his desk. "This company has treated them like crap for years. It's not fair."

"H3RO consistently underperform at every opportunity," Sejin told me, irritation radiating off him.

"You don't give them any opportunities," I snapped back at him. "There are no songwriters, no producers, and when I checked this morning, no recording studios."

Sejin unbuttoned his jacket and sat down. "Holly, you have to move quickly in this industry. There were recording slots available yesterday."

"Yes, now booked up with Cupcake who have only just finished recording their next comeback. They can wait a couple of months before getting back in the studio. How the hell are those girls going to fit it all in around their promotions? Promotions, which, I might add, have not been offered up to H3RO."

"H3RO don't have an album to promote yet," Sejin was quick to shoot back at me. "I am not wasting money on booking them on shows when they will fail to deliver a comeback."

"How are we going to get anything recorded if you refuse to give us studio time?" I retorted. "If the company's studios are booked up, the least you can do is increase the budget so we can use an external studio."

"The budget has been set based on their previous financial performances. If they want a bigger budget next time, they need to provide results this time," Sejin continued. "That's just business, nothing personal."

I slammed my foot down. "Yes, and sometimes you've got to spend money to make money."

Sejin sat back in his chair and fixed me a truly patronizing smile. "Sister, if it's too much for you, you can always quit now. I can't find the budget for external studio time, but I will personally buy you a first-class ticket back to Chicago."

"I'm not a quitter," I told him, firmly. I was pissed. That just made me more determined to wipe the smirk from his face. I turned on my heel and walked out of the room, keeping my head held high.

I had just stepped in the elevator and was hammering the button to go down when someone slipped in, just before the doors closed. I looked up, surprised it was Sejin's secretary, Park Inhye. She gave me a nervous smile. "I overheard your conversation," she told me.

I slumped against the wall. "Great."

"I went to school with Tae," she told me with a nervous shake of her head. "I know what Sejin says about him, but he is talented. When Hanjoo started he did try to fight for them, but your brother—"

"—Half-brother," I quickly corrected her. It was painful enough to acknowledge that much.

"Sejin would shoot him down. He gave up years ago." She grabbed my hand and pushed something into it. I looked down at a slip of paper and a car key in confusion. "It's the address of the company retreat. It's a few hour's drive from here, but I do know that it's not being used for the next few weeks."

"OK," I said, still confused.

"It has a recording studio in it," Inhye added as the elevator doors pinged open. Without looking at me, she darted out, leaving me staring after her. As the doors started to close, I stuck my hand out, catching it so I could escape myself.

I had at least one ally in Atlantis.

H3R☮

Although it was only lunch time, I was already exhausted—and starving. I picked up some fried chicken on the way back to the dorm, getting enough to hopefully feed the group as well. What I wasn't expecting when I walked in was the awkward, heavy atmosphere. All six members were in the small living area. Not one was looking at another and there wasn't any conversation.

I looked around the room in confusion as all six guys stared at me. "What did I miss?" I asked.

"A bunch of talentless guys arguing," Kyun snapped at me.

"Nobody said that, Kyun," Tae sighed. He looked weary but was still retaining his patience for his friend.

"Except Kyun," JunK muttered.

"Don't talk to me like that!" Kyun snapped, striding over to JunK.

"You're fifteen days older than me!" JunK barked back, standing up and squaring his chest off to the slightly older, very much taller and broader member.

"Whoa, guys!" Nate cried, leaping between the two of them with his arms outstretched, beating me to it. "Let's not fight!"

"I brought chicken?" I offered. "Can we discuss this over food?" Kyun shot me a murderous look and then stormed off. Seconds later, the door to the room he shared with Tae slammed shut. "Did I offend him with chicken?" I asked, half joking. The room remained silent. "Did I?"

"Kyun doesn't eat meat," Tae muttered before hurrying after him.

"Oh," I muttered, feeling dejected. So much for a pick-me-up chicken treat. I wasn't even hungry anymore; my appetite leaving with Kyun. I walked over to the table and set the bags down on it. "If anyone else eats chicken, there's plenty here." I kneeled, wishing I had put some pants on so I could sit more comfortably than I was currently with the dress suit I was wearing.

While I was moping, Minhyuk came and sat beside me, taking the many boxes of chicken out of the bag. "I haven't had chicken in months," he declared, selecting a box and pulling out a honey leg. "I will eat the whole lot if no one else will."

"Fight you for it," Dante said with a grin, sitting on the other side of me, pulling the spicy chicken out of Minhyuk's reach.

"Save me some," JunK muttered, heading to the kitchen.

I watched as he opened a cupboard and pulled out a pot of ramyun. I glanced at Dante, pulling a face. "Kyun loves ramyun," he said, not bothering to lower his voice. "That's JunK's way of apologizing."

"Is there anyone else with any dietary requirement I should be made aware of?" I asked with a sigh.

"I need to eat meat at least once a week," Nate grinned, taking a seat at the table and picking out his own box. "With beer. There must always be beer." When I stared at him, he winked. The simple action was like waving a magic wand and I felt relief wash over me.

At least they didn't *all* hate me.

A short while later, JunK disappeared with the pot of ramyun. When he returned to the room, both Tae and Kyun were with him. As though nothing had happened, the three sat down at the table, Tae and JunK reaching for a box of chicken each.

"When you've all finished eating, go and pack a bag," I announced.

The easy conversation that was being held evaporated. "We're leaving?" Kyun asked, going pale.

"Yes," I said. As his face went even paler, I realized how they were interpreting my words and I quickly put my hands up, waving them at the group. "No, not like that. We're going on a trip. I've got the Atlantis retreat for a couple of weeks. I thought it would be a good place to go to get away from here and hopefully find some inspiration for the album."

JunK and Nate looked at each other. "Holiday!" they yelled simultaneously, giving each other a high-five.

"It's not really a holiday, though," I pointed out. "It's work. We have an album to make."

Excitement seemed to fill the air and the chicken (and ramyun) was quickly devoured. While Minhyuk stayed behind to clear up, the others disappeared to pack a bag. "Do you think a change of location will help?" he asked me, pulling his hair back into a stubby ponytail.

I shrugged. "Given the frosty atmosphere when I walked in, it can't be much worse. If it's that bad, I can bring us back."

제4 장

H3R으

Playground

The company cabin was just outside of the Chiaksan National Park in Gangwon Province. The area was stunning. Fresh air filled my lungs. The national park was home to many peaks that lined the horizon, each covered in trees and vegetation. The different shades of green were a welcome difference to the artificial landscape of Seoul.

This place had to give the guys inspiration—*I* was inspired, and we'd only just arrived!

After a detour to get groceries, it was already late afternoon before we pulled up. Cabin wasn't really the right term. It was more of a country home than a cabin, but it was secluded in the woods. I was taking Inhye out for barbeque and soju when we got back. The girl had pulled through.

Inside, there were six bedrooms. I was ready to volunteer to take one of the couches, but Tae had announced he was sharing with Kyun and had gone to claim their room. I watched them leave with mild interest. I hadn't picked up on any kind of vibe from either of them, but I was starting to wonder just how far their relationship went and just what it entailed.

And then I shook my head. Whether those two were something or not, it wasn't my place to guess. Soon enough, their fandom would be speculating over who had a bromance and who had a romance anyway. There was no need for me to do that too.

I let the others pick their rooms while I unloaded the groceries from the car. With seven mouths to feed for a week, there were a lot of trips. It also hadn't been cheap. There really wasn't any money to spare in the ridiculously low budget we had, so I had used my own money to pay for the food.

Woojin had been giving me a weekly allowance of the place he'd found me which covered double the amount of the rent. I hadn't spent it on anything else and it had been mounting up. It wasn't enough for studio time, but as far as I was concerned, paying it back towards H3RO was the least I could do.

It wasn't long before I was joined by JunK. He sauntered over and leaned against the door frame, watching me. "I took your bags up," he informed me.

I gave him a grateful smile. "Thank you."

"You're in the room next to mine," he continued. "Just in case you get scared and you want someone to hold onto at night."

I paused in emptying the groceries into the fridge and rolled my eyes. "I'm a big girl. I can sleep by myself. I've managed to survive on my own for quite some time now."

JunK's lips quirked up and he took a few steps into the kitchen, stopping in front of me. "You're single then?"

"Thank god," I muttered. "I'm not sure how I'd explain to a boyfriend why I was sharing a house with six good-looking guys."

The smile turned into a smirk. "You think I'm good looking?"

I rolled my eyes again but didn't respond. Instead, I stepped around him and started to fill a cupboard with pots of ramyun; I had made sure that there would be plenty for Kyun, just in case there were other things he didn't like to eat.

"Hyung!" JunK cried, enthusiastically.

I looked over and found Minhyuk coming in, grinning at JunK. "Junnie," he returned.

"Holly thinks I'm good-looking."

I let out an impatient sigh and fixed JunK a disapproving look. "I said you were all good-looking," I corrected him.

"You still think I'm good-looking!" he announced, still smirking.

"Stop bothering our manager," Dante chided, joining us in the quickly filling kitchen. Despite the fact we were in the middle of nowhere and the only people he would see were us, his hair was immaculately styled, his long bangs held up and to the side with gel. Come to think of it, it had already been styled at breakfast earlier that morning.

I snorted. "He's not bothering me." I gave JunK my own smirk. "He can, however, finish putting the groceries away because I want to change and head outside into that beautiful mountain air. Which one is my room?"

"Second from the end," JunK replied.

It earned him a smack to the back of the head

from Dante. "That's your room."

"The last one," JunK grumbled, rubbing the back of his head. I laughed, leaving the three guys alone to finish the unpacking.

True to his word, JunK had brought my case up to my room for me. While I was technically still working, I was not in the office. I changed out of my work dress and pulled on a prettier summer one, more suitable for the sunny weather. I left my slippers in my room—I preferred to be barefooted where possible—and making sure I had grabbed my iPad and my sunglasses, I returned downstairs.

The house was empty. I looked around with a frown. The sliding doors at the far side of the room were open, so I walked over. As I got closer, I heard their animated chatter. Outside was a sheltered area with a large table. Behind that, a row of sun loungers. Behind that were H3RO, all acting like a bunch of excitable school children.

I joined Minhyuk's side, ready to ask what they were excited about, and spotted the pool. It was, large, deep, and …

"It's heated!" Nate yelled. He had been crouched down beside it, his foot extended to the water. Before he could put his foot back on dry land, JunK had gone charging over and shoved him. Nate went flying head first into the pool, sending a wave of water everywhere. I joined in the laughter as Nate resurfaced, yelling curses at JunK. *Really*? He should have seen that coming!

I picked out a sun lounger underneath a parasol and set my iPad on it as I started winding the parasol open. "Let me help," Dante offered, replacing my hand with his on the wheel. I stepped back and let him.

"Are you going to be joining them?" I asked, nodding over to Kyun and Tae who were kicking their flip flops off and getting into the pool with Nate.

"I didn't bring a swimsuit with me," he responded.

"Why should that stop you?" I asked. Judging from what Tae, JunK, and Nate were wearing in the water, it shouldn't have been too much of a problem. The weather was warm enough that the clothes would dry out quickly when hung out.

He cocked his head. "Are you suggesting I go skinny-dipping?" My eyes widened. That thought hadn't even crossed my mind. And then visions of him standing naked in front of me again were in the forefront of my thoughts. "Are you imaging me naked right now?" he asked, smirking. "Because I imagine you naked all the time."

"Actually, yes, I was," I shrugged, settling myself down on the lounger. "You can either go skinny dipping or keep your clothes on, because I've already got a memory of you naked in here, remember?" I responded, tapping the side of my head. I was rather surprised at my own boldness, but I wasn't lying. It was also worth it to see the look of astonishment on Dante's face.

"Are you coming?" Tae called over.

"I want to be," Dante called back, though his eyes were fixed firmly on me.

I wish I had been able to keep my composure at his innuendo, but I failed, my mouth falling open. Achieving the result he'd set out to get, Dante wiggled his eyebrows at me, and then sauntered off to the pool, pulling off his shirt. Finally, I had a clear view of the tattoo on his back. Or nearly clear: it was a Chinese dragon. The head dipped just below his shorts, but the body stretched out, up along his back, with the tail curling over his shoulder. It was mainly black with green and red highlights and as his muscles rippled, it gave the impression it was moving.

Dante flung his shirt back at me, where it landed on my calves, and then dove into the pool. Holy hell, that guy had my heart racing.

I pulled my sunglasses down, hiding behind the reflective lenses so I could watch H3RO. The four in the pool were trying to coax the other two in. Tae was the only one wearing a T-shirt, I noted. It did nothing to hide his muscles, however. Wet T-shirts do tend to stick, *in all the right places.* Of the six, these were the four that clearly spent the most time in the gym. Not that Kyun or Minhyuk were overweight or anything—they just had slim figures, and that didn't make them any less gorgeous.

I sighed and reached for my iPad. I was their manager. There was no point in wasting time looking because none of them should ever see me as anything other than that. I had to keep it professional because I was not going to allow Sejin the opportunity to cancel any contracts—H3RO's or mine.

No, I could do nothing more than watch the eye candy.

I flicked my iPad on and buried myself in work. I still had so much to learn about this industry.

H3RO

"Here," Nate said, sticking a bottle of water under my nose. I pulled my attention away from the iPad and

J. S. Lee

stared bleary eyed at him. He plucked the iPad away
from me and replaced it with the bottle, ignoring my
protests. "You're going to hurt your eyes."

I pushed the sunglasses to the top of my head and
rubbed at my eyes. "It's a bit late for that," I muttered.
I took a few mouthfuls of the cold liquid, then reached
up to rub at a kink in my neck.

Seconds later, my hand was swatted away by
Nate. "Move down," he ordered. I wrinkled my nose at
him but did as he said. When I had shuffled far enough
forward for him, he slipped in behind me. Then he was
massaging my neck and shoulders. "You need to sit up
properly too," he chided me.

My head lolled forwards. His touch was like hot
magic. "Priorities," I mumbled. "H3RO's album is
more important."

"Not really," Nate disagreed. "And there's no
reason why you can't sit properly and work on your
iPad."

"I'm a sloucher." I relaxed into his massage. "I've
always sat at a weird angle. When I was at college, I
would work in my bed rather than the desk. I don't
know why. It's just more comfortable." I looked up,
realizing it had gone quiet. "Where is everyone?"

"Inside," Nate replied. "We agreed that we were
going to get started on the album tomorrow. Minhyuk
and Kyun are cooking dinner. Tae and Dante went to
find the studio."

"Meanwhile, you're out here giving me a
massage," I said.

Nate paused. "I'm giving you a backrub, but I can
give you a massage if you want to lie down?"

If that had come from Dante, I would have been

questioning the level of innuendo in that offer. Instead, I glanced over my shoulder with an appreciative grin. "Don't worry about me," I told him. "I'm used to spending time in stupid positions on a laptop. Besides, there's a lot of work to be done."

"I think you're working too hard."

I shook my head. "What I'm doing is nothing in comparison to what you guys are going to have to do. That much I do know." I pushed the iPad away from me and shuffled away from Nate's body so I could stand up and stretch. "What I do need to do is make sure I get up and walk around a little more. Conveniently, I guess, my iPad needs charging."

I scooped the device up and headed inside. The kitchen was noisy. Minhyuk and Kyun were in the kitchen cooking something up, as Nate had said. I wasn't sure what, but it smelled delicious. I glanced at the giant clock which hung in the kitchen and did a double take. I hadn't realized how late it had gotten. No wonder I was so tired and hungry.

"What's cooking, good looking?" I called over, forgetting to speak Korean. Minhyuk looked confused, but Kyun seemed to understand.

"Sundubu-jjigae," Kyun responded. Tofu soup.

"It smells delicious," I said, remembering to reply in the right language.

Minhyuk gave me a bright smile. "It is nearly ready," he informed me.

I nodded, holding my iPad up. "I'm going to get this charging and then I'll be back," I promised him.

"Could you find Tae and Dante?"

"Of course," I called over my shoulder. I hurried upstairs, dropped the iPad into the docking station, and then started looking for the two eldest members of H3RO. I quickly established they weren't on the top floor. Hadn't Nate said they were looking for a studio?

I had done a quick loop of the ground floor: as well as the kitchen, there was a large, open living room, and a gym. Frowning to myself, I headed outside. When we had pulled up, I had spotted a building I had assumed was a garage, but maybe that was the studio.

I didn't get the chance to go in as the door opened and the two walked out. Neither looked happy. "Is everything OK?"

Tae shook his head. "Plenty of instruments, most of which need tuning, and no recording equipment."

I raked my hands through my hair. That put a dampener on things. How were they going to get anything recorded? "Don't worry," I told them, fixing a more positive expression on my face. "You guys worry about writing the music and the lyrics, and I'll get us a recording studio."

Tae looked doubtful but didn't comment.

How the hell was I going to get them in a recording studio now? Just another thing to add to my list of things to accomplish.

I followed the two back into the kitchen. Minhyuk and Kyun were no longer in there. Nor was the food. We went back outside to the poolside, finding the other members of H3RO already seated at the largest table, but none had started eating.

"About time," JunK declared as we drew near. "I thought I was going to starve!"

That earned him a clip around the ear from Tae as he walked past him to sit next to Kyun.

My stomach grumbled and I quickly took a seat

at the head of the table. Moments later, Minhyuk pushed a steaming bowl of soup in front of me. The table fell silent as we all started eating. Apparently, the fresh air and the swimming had worked up everyone's appetites. As several of them went back for second helpings, I was beginning to wonder if we had bought enough food to start with.

From the depths of my dress, something vibrated. Part of the reason I loved this dress so much was that it had pockets. Not enough of them did, and I found it irritating to carry my phone around all the time. I pulled the phone out—it was an email. I quickly read it, growing excited, and for the first time hopeful.

"What are you looking so pleased about?" JunK asked.

When I looked up, I realized everyone was looking at me. "I don't want to jinx it, so I'm not going to share the details," I told them. "But I have just confirmed a very important meeting first thing tomorrow, so I'm going to have to leave you unsupervised tonight."

"Why?" JunK asked.

This time, he got a dig in the ribs from Nate. "She *just* said she wasn't going to share the details."

"Tease," JunK muttered in my direction.

"Is it about us?" Tae asked, quietly. Tae was very softly spoken. Given how boisterous the others could get, I was surprised at how he was never ignored. It was like they were always listening out for him, and he always had their attention when he did speak. I liked it.

I nodded. "But it's nothing to worry about."

"I will go with you," Tae decided.

I gave him a smile and shook my head. "You

should be here, working on the album."

"You shouldn't be driving to Seoul alone. It's already late," he disagreed. "And it's not up for discussion."

"We can get started without Tae," Minhyuk agreed.

Given that only a few hours ago, instead of creating they were bickering and calling each other talentless, I wasn't sure how successful it was going to be. Nonetheless, there was something about Tae which left me feeling like he was coming with me no matter what I said.

It was a breakfast meeting, and even if we were there a couple of hours, we could still be back by lunchtime. I looked to Tae and shrugged. "We should probably leave soon."

"Finish eating first," he instructed me.

I don't know why, but I listened. I picked my spoon back up and finished the soup Minhyuk had made. He really had talent in the kitchen.

H3RO

I wasn't entirely sure why Tae had insisted on coming back to Seoul with me. He didn't say a word the whole way back. He did however, sit in the front of the small minibus with me, rather than somewhere in the back, but the silence was kept at bay with the radio.

It wasn't until we were back in the dorm that he spoke. I had pulled a bottle of water from the fridge and settled down on the couch. I was exhausted from the driving and I wanted to have a half hour of doing nothing before going to bed.

"Is the meeting tomorrow about H3RO?" Tae asked, suddenly.

I had been staring out of the window, trying to see if I could see anything in the buildings opposite with their lights on. I turned back to the room I was in. Tae was standing in front of the small television, staring down at me. "Huh?"

"The meeting tomorrow," he repeated. "Is it about us?"

I nodded. "Yes. But I told you that back in Chiaksan."

"Are you going to disband us?" he demanded.

I stared up at him. Although his words were blunt and his face stern, he looked like he was trying not to cry. I stood up and walked over to him. "Tae, I am absolutely not going to a meeting to discuss your disbandment. The meeting is with a company called KpopKonneKt. I don't know if you've heard of them, but they run projects. Fundraising projects. It's like Kickstarter, but for K-Pop. It has a largely international audience, but people pledge different amounts." I reached for his hand and gave him a smile. "I'm trying to get us money to make this album—and the music video!"

Tae pulled his hands free, but he didn't move away. He continued to stare down at me. "They're my family," he finally whispered. "H3RO. We've been together for over eight years. It can't end this way. I don't know what else we will do."

"It's not going to end this way," I assured him. Tae turned away and I sighed, darting in front of him, thinking I had upset him. I had, but not in the way I had thought. He was crying. "Tae!" I exclaimed.

"I'm fine," he muttered, trying to get around me.

I stepped back to let him get to his room. I could feel the tears welling up in my own eyes. Was I capable of doing this? The lives of six men were depending on me not fucking this up. Once again, I was reminded that I was in way over my head and that thought terrified me.

제5 장

H3R으

Really Really

I was awake, staring at the ceiling. I had been tossing and turning for most of the night, terrified that I was going to screw the meeting up—screw everything up. I had gone from not wanting to be in Korea, not wanting to know Lee Woojin, not wanting anything to do with his company, to ... well, I still didn't give a crap about Lee Woojin. He could try to be my father all he wanted, but he hadn't been there for any of the twenty-four years of my life, so I didn't really care.

But somehow, I had become invested in H3RO. It was kind of concerning that it had only been a few days too, but right then, their future was my priority. I wasn't sure where the reputation of them being troublemakers at Atlantis had come from, but they all seemed like genuinely decent guys. Guys, who, like Tae, really wanted to succeed and weren't, solely because of my stupid-ass half-brother who didn't like them enough to support them.

I had found a reason to stay in Korea *and* to work at Atlantis—for now, at least. In some ways, it was nice to have a goal. Mainly, it was terrifying considering the stakes.

When morning eventually rolled around, I had managed to grab a few hours of broken sleep. As it was still early, I took a quick shower before Tae woke up, and pulled on a smart dress. By the time Tae appeared, I was pacing back and forth between the TV and the couch.

I glanced over and did a double take. *Holy Hell!* He was wearing a deep blue suit and I had the strongest urge to get him out of it.

Professionalism, Holly!

I quickly cleared my throat, pushing that thought from my mind. "Are you coming with me?"

"If it relates to H3RO, I'd like to," Tae said. His tone was firm, but I could see him balling his hands into fists like he was trying to build his courage.

I gave him my brightest smile. "I would love it if you did," I told him. "It would be nice for KpopKonneKt to see who they could be working with." I glanced at my watch. We had arranged to meet at their offices on the other side of the city and with it being a breakfast meeting, it wouldn't hurt to leave. "We should go now though," I told him.

We walked in silence to the parking lot. It wasn't until we reached the Range Rover that Tae spoke, and when he did, he was confused. "Who does this belong to?"

"Lee … my father bought it for me as a guilt present," I said, cringing as I said father. "I thought it would appear more professional if we took this instead of the minibus." I glanced over at the vehicle in question on the other side of the lot. It was parked amongst a dozen other newer-model minibuses. *Much* newer. It didn't surprise me anymore.

Tae nodded and got in the passenger side. He waited until the exit barriers let us out before speaking again. "You don't get on with your father?"

I shook my head. "It's not that I don't. I don't know him. I don't want to know him though. He's rich," I sighed. "When my mom got pregnant with me, she wasn't deemed suitable for him. Aside from the fact that he was married, my grandparents were farmers from just outside of Daegu so they weren't socializing in the same circles. My mom got chased out of the country. He never once enquired about me until earlier this year and now he thinks he has control over my life."

"You don't want to be here then?"

I shot him a sideways glance. "I didn't," I admitted. "I argued with my mom for weeks about coming out here. I grew up in a non-Asian area outside of Chicago. The only Asians there were my mom, who ran the Korean restaurant, and the Chinese family who ran the Chinese restaurant. Talk about walking clichés." I sighed and slowed to allow a car to pull out. "My mom didn't want me getting bullied at school for being different, so she didn't speak much Korean at home." I laughed, the sound making my mouth feel bitter. "She learned English for me. She could have gone to any city with a decent Korean community, but she hid away in the suburbs of Chicago because my *father* broke her heart and threw her out. So, no, I didn't want to come here."

"What about now?" he asked. I frowned and gave him another sideways look. He was staring ahead out of the window, keeping his gaze fixed on the car in front.

But that insecurity was there again.

I really was going to kick Lee Sejin's ass for his treatment of this group.

"My goal is to get you guys a kick-ass album and a number one!" I said. "I'm going nowhere until that happens."

"What happens if that happens?"

"When."

"If it happens," Tae repeated. "The number one."

"No, I mean *when*," I said again. "*If* is a probability. *When* is a certainty." I felt Tae staring at me, and when I turned my head, he was. "What?"

"You really believe in us?"

"You bet I do," I confirmed with finality, leaving no room for argument.

H3RO

KpopKonneKt was on the floor above a pancake house. From the outside it didn't look particularly special, but the inside was bright and modern. It was a small, open-plan office with about a half dozen staff. They were busy working at their own workstations, but the atmosphere was relaxed and casual. I was starting to feel overdressed in my outfit compared to their jeans and sneakers.

"Miss Holly Lee?"

I turned finding a man maybe a little older than Tae staring questioningly at me. "Woo Byungho?" He gave me a bright smile and bowed. I bobbed my head before accepting his hand to shake.

"Mr. Park Hyuntae," he greeted Tae. "I recognize you from your videos." Tae looked momentarily startled at that but recovered quickly in greeting Woo Byungho. "I have a meeting room set up for us, this way." He gestured down a corridor before leading us to the room he was referring too.

The first thing I noticed was the pile of pancakes in the middle of the room. I don't know why, but just by seeing them, I knew this was going to be a good meeting.

"Before we start, why don't you help yourself to something to eat," Woo Byungho suggested. He could probably see me drooling over them.

I didn't need telling twice, taking some and covering them with a healthy drowning of syrup. I took a seat and started eating while Woo Byungho started his introductory spiel. By the time I had finished, so had he.

"Of the three years we've been running this, we've only ever had two artists be unsuccessful on their first attempt. There have been occasions where we've had to extend the goal deadline, but for the most part, many artists have surpassed the goal set by at least fifty percent." Woo Byungho leaned forward, resting his elbows on the table. "The more you can provide for each set, the better the rewards, the more people around the world will be willing to commit. Even for groups they've not heard of."

I was sure he was saying that in a pleasant *FYI* manner, but I could feel Tae tense up beside me. I started to reach over to give his hand a squeeze but stopped myself: he hadn't been brought up in America and skinship was a big deal for him.

"Now, for the important part, if I might ask: what figure are you looking at setting as a goal?"

I blew out a breath. Considering the size of

Atlantis, this was going to be embarrassing. However, some things were more important than my own pride, and frankly, it should be Atlantis who was ashamed, not me or H3RO. Besides, if the project went live, Tae and H3RO were going to find out anyway. "Ten million won." About nine thousand dollars.

I could feel both Tae and Woo Byungho stare at me in astonishment. "*Aigoo!*" Woo Byungho exclaimed under his breath.

"Atlantis has invested most of the budget in post marketing," I said. That wasn't exactly a lie. What I didn't mention was the size of that budget … "I mean, I could lower that figure, but I would be cutting corners that I don't want to cut."

"While the figure is extraordinarily high," Woo Byungho hurried to assure me. "We've had groups set that figure and still surpass it. You must forgive my surprise, I just wasn't expecting that from Atlantis."

"SM, YG, JYP, and Atlantis … I bet you weren't ever expecting any of those entertainment companies to turn up at your door," I sighed. I raked a hand through my hair, doing my best to ignore the stare Tae was boring into the side of my head. "Look, H3RO haven't had a comeback in two years, and the last one wasn't as successful as Atlantis wanted it to be. They've been focusing their efforts mostly into Onyx, B.W.B.B., and Cupcake. I want H3RO to have the best comeback they've had to date. They deserve it, and their fans deserve it. So, if I'm setting that figure that high, it's because I have the confidence they will achieve it, and that we can deliver what is promised."

"I don't doubt they will," Woo Byungho agreed. "If I might offer up some advice? Work on your SNS presence. H3RO will need to keep providing updates, doing so gets participants and potential participants engaged. Give them as much as you can. Let them get to know H3RO."

"Thank you," I said, holding in the sigh I wanted to let escape. Working on their SNS—Social Networking Service, as social media was referred to out here—would be easy enough.

"I will draw up the contract and have it couriered to Atlantis this afternoon."

"Please can you send it to Chiaksan? We're at the company retreat working on the album," I quickly requested. I didn't want this getting to Lee Sejin just yet.

"Leave the details with my secretary," he agreed.

We said our goodbyes, dropped the information off with the secretary and left the KpopKonneKt offices. For the whole drive back to the dorm apartment, I was feeling elated. We still had a long way to go, and a mountain's worth of work to complete, but for the first time, I genuinely felt more positive that we could do it.

We quickly grabbed our things from the apartment. This time I made sure to stuff a bikini in my case and then hurried down to the minibus. I put my case in the back alongside Tae's and had just shut the door when all of a sudden, a hand was on each shoulder and I was being forced back against the door. "Tae!" I cried, trying to shake myself free of his grasp.

He released me but didn't step back. "Are you here to disband us?"

I shook my head. "I don't know how many times I have to tell you this, but I'm here for a comeback and a number one. The last thing I have any intention of doing is disbanding you."

"Then why is the KPopKonneKt campaign figure so high?"

"Because I want H3RO to have the best comeback they can. Because I know that you can hit that figure. Because you guys have been screwed over by Atlantis so many times in the past that I want us to be able to do this without their help and so I can say a massive 'fuck you' to Lee Sejin!" I cried. "If the only way I can do that is to ask your fans for help, then I'm going to do it. It's my pride on the line, not yours. If this goes wrong, I will personally stand in front of the world's media and issue a statement that it was my fault: you had a manager that fucked up."

I stared up at him, refusing to break the stare, even though it was growing increasingly uncomfortable. Tae's dark eyes were fixed on mine. They were intense: angry, troubled … sad.

"Please don't hurt H3RO," he finally begged, his voice breaking as he spoke. "I wasn't lying. This is my family. This is my past, my present, and my future. If you take that away, I don't have anything."

Before I could stop myself, I reached up and gently cupped his cheek. "I'm going to do *everything* I possibly can to restart your career, Tae. The last thing I plan to do is break up the group."

Tae stared back at me, then suddenly jerked his head from my hand and stepped back. Without a word, he pulled open the door to the front passenger seat and got in.

I stood where I was for a moment, trying to calm myself. He hadn't scared me, but he had startled me. From a distance, or at least from the photographs and music videos I had seen, Tae had a naturally dark expression. Up close, I could see that darkness was more of a sadness than anything else. Sadness and a fierce need to protect his chosen family.

My racing heart wasn't from his actions.

It was due to the increasing levels of pressure being set on me.

H3RO's comeback was more important than anything else and I could not fuck this up.

제6 장

H3R으

War of Hormone

The drive back was longer than it needed to be. We hit traffic getting out of the city, and then got stuck behind *two* different wrecks. What should have taken a couple of hours took double that. The whole time was spent with nothing but silence to keep us company. Or keeping *me* company.

That didn't bother Tae. He just plugged in his earphones and pointedly stared out of the other window.

At least the radio still worked.

By the time we got to the retreat, I was tired and cranky. The earlier elation at getting the KpopKonneKt campaign had worn off. Without the ability to multitask driving and working, I had resorted to creating a mental checklist of things to accomplish. The first was to take another look at the SNS as Woo Byungho had suggested.

I was still lost in thought when JunK all but pounced on me when we walked through the door with my bags. "Are you going to tell us what your meeting was about now?" I blinked, looking around. Everyone was waiting for us.

I started to nod, but I caught the expression on Kyun's face. He was staring behind me and he looked disappointed. I glanced over my shoulder and found Tae there, refusing to look in my direction, but his face said nothing but failure.

"Yes," I said, firmly. "But I need something cold to drink because that was a long drive back and I'm really thirsty." I walked calmly to the fridge and pulled a bottle of water from it. "Let's go sit outside." Without waiting to see if they were following me, I walked outside and straight to the large table we had been using to eat at. I took a seat, and one by one, the group sat themselves down around me.

I could tell they were anxious to hear what had happened, but I had to gulp some liquid down first. "I went to meet with KpopKonneKt. They're kind of a fundraising organization aimed specifically at K-Pop groups. It has a huge international fan reach. They agreed to take us on for this album project."

"Why would you need to go to KpopKonneKt?" Kyun asked, his eyes narrowing with suspicion.

I had been deliberating how I was going to answer this the entire drive here. The easiest thing would be to lie, to keep the peace for a while longer, until after the comeback. By then, we'd have been successful so it wouldn't be an issue. But that would rely on Tae not saying anything, and he was too loyal to his group for me to ask him to do that. Plus, I didn't want to put him in that position.

I opted for the truth.

"Because, honestly, the budget assigned to this

comeback isn't enough. But also, because this will give you an opportunity to reach more international fans. These are the amazingly loyal people who will buy your albums, watch your videos, and share your posts. Doing a KpopKonneKt campaign is a wonderful way to connect with them."

"I don't speak English," Kyun said, suddenly looking terrified.

I quickly shook my head. "I'm not forcing you to speak English," I promised him. "You speak Korean. I'll work with KpopKonneKt to sub your videos. Same with the V Live and if—"

"We get a V Live?" JunK blurted out.

I looked at him, surprised at how giddy with excitement he was with that. "You guys don't have a V Live?" I asked, slowly. V Live was a video streaming service designed specifically for idols and celebrities to stream to their fans. Groups would have their own page where they could also provide other content, but it mainly allowed for a live chat at the same time: fans would type out their messages and the idol could respond in the video.

"Our contracts say no social media unless approved by the company," Dante shrugged. "We're still waiting on that."

"Nothing?" I asked, my eyes going wide.

"We have a Twitter account, but Shin Hanjoo controlled it," Minhyuk chimed in. "Are we really going to be allowed an account? Personal ones?"

I was about to say yes, but opposite me, Tae caught my eye. He gave one, very subtle, shake of his head. "H3RO will definitely be getting SNS accounts," I responded. "Let me get back to you on the personal ones." As JunK and Minhyuk high-fived each other, I frowned. "And they're going to come with guidelines, you know, like not posting inappropriate crap," I said, my tone dry. "But this is stuff you don't need to worry about. You guys just need to work on this album, and I'll work on everything else."

I grabbed my bottle and headed back inside. I took my bag up to my room and collected my iPad while I was there, that way I could start writing down the to-do list that was in my head before I forgot something. While there, I changed out of my suit, into a summery dress. With the iPad under my arm, I stepped out of my room and almost walked into Tae. "Oh!" I gasped, stumbling back.

His hand shot out to steady me. He glanced down the corridor, and then, without any warning, leaned forward, bringing his face close to mine. "Tae?" I whispered, hardly daring to breath because of his close proximity. There was a click and the door opened behind me. Tae stared at me, until he finally nodded his head in the direction of my room. Flustered, I walked back in. He followed me, closing the door behind us and stood in front of it, continuing to stare down at me. "What?" I asked, still feeling embarrassed.

"Are you really not going to disband us?"

I sighed. "Are we really going to have this conversation again? Because I will get T-shirts printed up if I need to." When he didn't respond, I brought the iPad up to my chest and wrapped my arms around it. "I have absolutely *zero* intention of disbanding H3RO. My only goal right now is for you to have a successful comeback—one so successful that Atlantis will regret all the time they've wasted not doing this sooner."

"OK," Tae eventually responded. "I'm going to trust you on that." He continued to stare at me.

"Was there anything else?" I asked when it seemed like he wasn't going to leave.

"We need group SNS accounts," he said. It seemed more like a command than a request. "Don't let us have individual ones."

"Honestly, I was leaning that way anyway," I agreed. "I just got a little caught up in JunK and Minhyuk's excitement. Why don't you want an individual account like they do?" I asked, genuinely curious.

Instead of a response, Tae finally left the room.

I let a breath escape me. He was a very intense person and it could be draining sometimes. I did get it though. I'm sure Tae would be upset if he knew I was feeling this much pity for them, but this group were completely hard done by.

My eyes narrowed. With each passing hour, my resentment toward my 'family' and Atlantis Entertainment was growing. As was my intention of stealing the company away from them. I made another addition to my mental list; to check out the other groups and actors on the roster. I'd heard something being mentioned during the initial meeting I had attended, about the rookie group Bright Boys being a problem for the company, with one of the members potentially being sent for early enlistment because of a scandal he was supposedly caught up in. That would definitely need investigating … But first I needed to deliver Tae and the rest of H3RO the comeback I kept promising.

H3RO

I couldn't sleep. I had spent the day in front of my iPad and finally I had a schedule planned out. I knew rough timings of when each thing needed to be completed by and could now say for certain that the less-than two-month period that Sejin had given me was utterly ridiculous.

I'd also spent some time looking at the SNS situation. The only other group in a similar situation was Bright Boys, but until recently, when their leader had been caught up in a scandal, their SNS across all various platforms had been updated regularly by all the members, as well as staff. H3RO didn't even have a fandom name, or a fan café.

I was honestly questioning why they were ever debuted in the first place.

While checking in on my own Instagram account, I'd spotted some photos from a college friend, Kate. She had been touring around the US with a hugely successful popstar as the official photographer and had just wrapped up.

It was early morning in Las Vegas where she lived, but I dropped her a quick message asking her if she fancied a new challenge. Less than an hour later, I had her booked on a flight out to Seoul. Kate had agreed to fly out for a couple of weeks and do a few photoshoots for us—with a heavily discounted friend's rate.

We weren't anywhere near ready to shoot the album jacket just yet. I wanted it to match the feel of the video and I still had to find someone to shoot that for us. It didn't mean that we couldn't get some shots taken to put out there either on SNS or KpopKonneKt—or both.

By the time midnight rolled around, I was exhausted, but I could not get my brain to switch off. It wasn't very often that I got like this, but the only way to get through it was to wear myself out. Back home, I'd go to the twenty-four-hour gym that I was a member of. Although there was a gym in the cabin, I was more taken with the idea of a night swim, especially as I had brought my bikini with me.

I got out of bed and quickly changed into the simple black two-piece. I wrapped myself up in a dressing gown and then made my way downstairs without turning a light on. I wasn't sure how deeply the guys slept, and given they were determined to get up early and make a start on some songs, I didn't want to disturb their beauty sleep.

Outside it was blissfully peaceful. Aside from a few bugs and animals, the only real sound came from the breeze playing with the trees, and the gurgle of the water as it lapped against the side of the pool.

Discarding the robe on one of the sun loungers, I stretched and dove into the pool and began churning up and down with a front crawl. I lost track of the time and it wasn't until around my twentieth length that I decided to take a break.

I swam over to a small underwater ledge and sat down on it. Facing the side of the pool I realized I wasn't alone. "Did I wake you?" I asked JunK.

He shook his head, his gaze fixed firmly on me. "Our rooms overlook the pool," he explained, pointing up at the windows above us. "I saw you."

"Do you want to join me?" I asked, uncertainly. He was wearing a T-shirt and a pair of shorts, but I wasn't sure if it was his intention to swim, or just be outside. "Or is there something wrong?"

"Nothing's wrong," he said, shaking his head. He walked around to my side of the pool and sat down, dangling his legs in. "How can they afford to heat a pool when no one is here, but they can't give us a song?" he asked, bitterly.

"Tell me about it," I muttered, feeling as resentful as he did. "I'm sorry," I blurted out, feeling guilty about the way they had been treated by my own *flesh and blood*.

"Why?" he asked, tilting his head, confused.

"I ..." I stopped myself. Telling him who I was wouldn't help. "I wish I could do more," I finished without lying. I really did.

JunK slid into the water, joining me on the step, close enough that our arms were brushing. "I think Tae and Dante will be able to make some good songs for us," he said. "Dante has taught himself to play so many instruments, and Tae has been wanting to learn how to produce. I just don't want them to do badly, because if they do, I know they'll blame themselves."

I worried about that too. It wasn't that I thought that they, H3RO, wouldn't be able to create an amazing album. It was that I knew Atlantis wasn't going to help them get it out there. If no one knew about it, then how could anyone buy or stream it? KpopKonneKt would help, but Byungho himself had said they had more success with international fans than with domestic ones. I knew it wouldn't be enough on its own.

Instead of telling him all this, I stared out across the water, smiling. "You guys are going to nail it. Even you, JunK," I said, resolutely. I turned and found JunK staring at me. "What?"

"Please don't call me that."

"JunK?" I asked, frowning. "It's what the others call you?"

"Sejin chose it before we debuted," he said bitterly. "I didn't know what I was agreeing to until Nate laughed at me later about it. By then Sejin wouldn't let me change it."

I didn't say anything.

"In the beginning, all I would get were comparisons to 2PM's JunK or that I was trying to be him."

I had thought the same thing when I had first read through JunK's bio. I frowned thoughtfully. "If you don't like it, let's change it."

JunK blinked. "We can do that?"

I nodded. "I'm your manager. Besides, I'm going to be overseeing all the artwork. I'll just make sure that going forward everyone knows your new name, whatever that will be."

"It's not that I don't like it. It's just I don't want to keep being compared to JunK. I want to be me. I want to be Jun," he said. "Just Jun."

"Well, Just Jun," I teased, grinning. "Welcome to H3RO." It earned me a smile.

"We can really do this?" he asked.

I looked out over the water, watching the ripples lap against the far side of the pool. "We're doing this album by ourselves. We can do what we want, including name changes and makeovers. Sometimes you've just got to do it: find what you want and put yourself out there, before it's too late. Better to ask forgiveness than permission," I replied cheekily.

There was movement beside me and a slight splash of water as Jun dropped into the pool. He moved in front of me, staring at me with a strange intensity which was making me feel strangely exposed.

I didn't entirely dislike the feeling.

I cleared my throat attempting to distract both him and me. "You'd best not be thinking about dunking me in the water."

"That's not even close to what I'm thinking," Jun said, the words a low husky rumble. Jun had the deepest voice and hearing him sing was literal music to my ears. Right now, his voice was playing a different tune.

I cleared my throat again. "I'm not sure I want to ask."

Without warning, his hands were on my thighs, gliding up, over my hips to my waist where they clung on as Jun stepped closer. I let out an involuntary shiver. "You're beautiful," he murmured, leaning in towards me.

"What are you doing?" I whispered, even though it was very clear to me and anyone who saw us what he was doing.

"What I want to do," he murmured back.

I closed my eyes before I knew what I was doing. A second later and his lips were claiming mine. *Holy hell!* Jun was certainly acting like he knew what he wanted. My arms swung up, wrapping around his neck. When my hands started playing with the wet ends of his hair at the nape of his neck, he let out a small growl. The hands on my waist tightened, pulling me to him.

I gasped from the contact between our bodies, and then his tongue was massaging mine. He tasted of mint mixed with the chlorine from the water, and strangely, I couldn't get enough of it. I wrapped my legs around him, sending the water rolling away in choppy waves. The motion made him stumble, and I could feel one arm leave me to steady us, but his mouth never left mine. If anything, it only made him kiss me harder.

A moan escaped me and my legs tightened around his waist. I was both grateful for the water, and resenting it, as the cool temperature did its best to calm me down. Then both of Jun's hands were back on my body, sliding down me to my butt. They slid under, squeezing, then pulled me off the ledge. The motion had me releasing my grip and allowing my legs to fall. I slid down his body, not missing the fact that he was obviously as aroused as I was. As my feet touched the bottom of the pool, Jun stepped forwards, sandwiching me between the poolside and his body, with another grunt.

One of his hands left my butt, moving around to the front of my body, skimming over my hip. His fingers sliding between my skin and the bikini bottoms, tugging at the fabric. With great effort, I started to pull away. The moment I did, his hands dipped below the waistline, and around the curve of my body.

I froze, unable to command myself to move as a finger slipped inside me. Instead, my body responded by itself. I arched my back, a moan escaping my mouth. The moan morphed into a small cry as a second finger joined the first, while the heel of Jun's hand began rubbing up against my sensitive area. His heated movements, contrasting with the coolness of the water, were like nothing I'd ever experienced before. "Oh, god," I ground out as Jun increased the speed of his digits that were entering me. I clung at his shoulders, not caring how tight my grip was. I was so close. "Oh, god, Jun."

His fingers slowed, before he pulled them out of me. I opened my eyes, finding him smirking at me. "You want me to stop?"

"You're a bad maknae," I scolded him, my words holding little weight in between my desperate gasps. "Oh, holy hell," I moaned, this time not from pleasure. "You're the maknae. You're the baby."

"I'm twenty-three, Holly." Jun leaned forward, bringing his mouth to the side of my head. "I'm not that much younger than you, and I may be the *maknae*, but I have the power to do this," he muttered into my ear as he thrust his fingers back inside me.

I let out a moan of pleasure. Once again, my body was crying out for him and he was answering. *Oh, fuck it!* I relaxed into him and began rubbing myself against the heel of his hand. Once again, his movements slowed. "Don't. You. Dare!" I growled.

"Kiss me," he demanded or begged, I couldn't really tell at this point.

Anything to get his fingers working me again.

I leaned forward, doing as he wished. Thankfully, it worked. Harder, and faster, our tongues matching his fingers. And then he hit the sweet spot that was hidden within my body. His fingers continued working me as the cry escaped me. My legs felt like they were melting away beneath me, and it was only because of his hand and his still steady grip on my hip that I was able to stay upright.

When my body began to instinctively lean forward, wanting to ride out the blissful spasms his fingers continued to tease out of it, Jun moved his head. Once again, his mouth captured mine. At some point, his hand moved back to join the other, holding me up.

His kisses lessened in intensity and when I pulled away from him again, he allowed it.

I slumped forward, resting my head on his shoulder, breathing heavily.

That was much better than a workout at the gym.

The haze I was in started to wear off and I pushed myself away from Jun. "Oh, crap," I muttered.

"You feel better?" he asked me, his hands keeping a firm grip on my waist.

"I did," I responded, trying to wriggle away. "But we shouldn't have done that."

"I enjoyed that as much as you did," he declared.

"It's irrelevant. I'm your *manager*." I finally broke free and returned to the side of the pool, putting some distance between us. I clutched at the wall and closed my eyes. I was still riding high from his fingers and I couldn't seem to get my body to calm down. Everything was feeling hypersensitive in the water and the now cool night air.

I nearly jumped out of the water when Jun's hands slid back around me, pulling my back into his chest. "Being my manger is what's irrelevant," he murmured, his mouth close to my ear. It sent a shiver down my spine.

My body ignored the warnings I was sending it and relaxed backwards. "You're too young to know how to do that," I told him before I could stop myself. I was rewarded with his lips on my neck and a low, quiet chuckle. I let out a whimper. "Jun ..." His hand moved back down, sliding back below my bikini bottoms. "Jun!" I exclaimed, more firmly this time, reaching down to remove it. I spun around to glare at him, still holding his hand. "You can't do that."

He cocked his head. "You didn't enjoy it?"

"I did," I sighed. "I think that was pretty obvious. But that doesn't mean it should have happened."

"Who says?" Jun asked. I was still holding his hand away from me, while his other continued holding my waist. It was like we were frozen in some weird ballroom dance. He slowly lowered his head, giving me every opportunity to move mine.

I didn't.

Instead, I accepted his lips, and then his tongue. I finally released his captured hand, if only so I could wrap my arms once again around his neck. I found myself disappointed when his hand didn't return any lower than my waist. Then, before I knew what he was doing, he broke away. "Next time," he promised me before hauling himself out of the pool in one smooth movement which only served to show me a brilliant view of his back muscles under his wet shirt. He shot me a cheeky smirk, then *sauntered* his way back into the building.

제7 장

H3RO

Devil

For the next week, it was almost like nothing had ever happened between me and Jun. At breakfast, after Kyun called Jun 'JunK', I announced he was now going by Jun. Nate had muttered an "about time", but otherwise, it was an uneventful renaming ceremony.

But just when I'd start to think my brain had dreamed it all up, I'd catch Jun's eye and he'd give me that cheeky smirk. Every time it happened, I'd look at whoever else was around, wondering if they could tell that it meant 'I know exactly how to make you moan', but they all seemed oblivious. I was torn between wanting to punch him and wanting to drag him back for that second round.

Not that I had imagined anything with any of the members (OK, that's a lie—something may have briefly entertained my thoughts after seeing Dante naked), but I had never expected the *maknae* to be the problem.

I had hardly seen anything of Tae, Dante or Minhyuk. The three of them had all but moved into the recording studio. If it wasn't for the fact they appeared at meal times, I would have thought it was just three guys with me, and even then, the trio sometimes had to be called to eat several times.

If I'd have stayed in my room to work, I wouldn't have seen much of the other members myself. I had turned the inside dining table into my own desk, slowly spreading out over it as the days progressed.

"If something has been left here, does it mean we can use it?" Jun said, tearing my attention away from the monitor.

As I looked up, a bottle of water and a banana was thrust in front of my face. I took the items from Nate and flashed him a grateful smile. He was making sure I stayed hydrated. "What have you found?" I asked Jun.

From behind his back, he produced a camera. I stared at it: it looked newish. I looked to Jun and shrugged. "Don't break it."

Jun grinned, bringing it up to his eye to take a picture of Kyun who was seated at the table with me. I had set him the task of coming up with a list of things we could include as our KpopKonneKt campaign extras and he was taking it as seriously as our songwriters. Right now, his face was screwed up in concentration, one pen behind his ear, another in his mouth, and a third he was using to write with.

Watching Jun suddenly gave me a lightbulb moment. "Take as many photos as you want!" I declared happily. "We can launch your Instagram account later today and you can post some on there."

"I really get an Instagram account?" he exclaimed in excitement. It was followed up with a little jiggle of happiness.

Although that made me smile, I shook my head. "It will be a single group account, but you will all have access to it."

"Does that mean we get a phone too?" he asked. His excitement had dipped only fractionally, and now he was looking at me with pleading eyes.

Both Nate and Kyun turned their heads to listen to my answer. "You guys don't have phones?" I asked, surprised.

"Our contracts said that having phones were like having SNS: nothing until management agrees," Jun explained. He pulled out the chair next to me and sat down, placing the camera in front of him. "Please can we finally have a phone?"

"Hang on, doesn't Tae have a phone?" I asked, sure he had been on it on our way back from the KpopKonneKt meeting.

Nate shook his head. "It's an iPod. A *really* old one, with no internet access either. Tae really can't live without his music."

I frowned. "Oh … well, yes, you can have a phone, but I don't have the budget to be going out buying all of you the latest iPhone, so it will probably be one for you to share." I thought about it then shook my head. "Actually, you can have an iPad for now."

"I'll take that!" Jun cried, leaping to his feet and sending the chair flying. He grabbed the camera and hurried off.

"Will we be able to have phones?" Nate asked.

"Why, have you got a girlfriend you need to be texting?" I teased.

Nate looked me dead in the eye with a stare that

had me feeling hot around the collar, the raffish grin wasn't helping that either. "Not yet."

Whatever thought started going through my head evaporated as my phone rang. I glanced down, spotting Sejin's name. I let out a long sigh and picked the phone up. "Yes?"

"Get your ass in my office. Now."

That was it. The bastard hung up on me before I could question him. I glowered down at my phone, imagining it was a video call and that I had the ability to crawl through the screen and punch him square in the face.

"Is everything OK?" Nate asked.

"Family drama, it's fine," I muttered as I got to my feet.

Nate mimicked me. "You don't look fine. Where are you going?"

"I have a meeting at Atlantis," I told him. "With an asshole I really don't want to see."

"I'll come with you."

"Stay," I said, waving him back down (which he ignored). "I was going to be leaving in a couple of hours to pick up a friend from the airport, anyway. I'll just leave a little earlier."

"Who is he?" Nate asked, folding his arms.

I laughed. "He is a she. Kate. I went to college with her. She's coming to help us out."

"Is she a songwriter?" Nate asked, dubious.

"She's a photographer. She's just finished touring with a US popstar and conveniently has a couple of weeks to spare. I bribed her with a free holiday if she did some shots for us," I explained. "Her flight gets in this evening."

Nate tightened his arms over his chest and frowned at me. "Where is she going to sleep?"

"She can have my room," I shrugged, realizing I hadn't thought of that. "I'll go—"

"You can share my bed," Jun said. I hadn't even realized he was back in the room and I jumped backwards—bumping straight into him.

"I don't ... think ..." I spluttered at the look he was giving me. It was that same one he had been giving me all week: that 'I know how to make you moan' look. "I don't think so!" I finally declared. I stepped away, cursing myself as I shivered like my body was remembering his touch. "I need to go," I muttered, hurrying out of the room.

Outside in the fresh air, I took several deep breaths. What happened in the pool shouldn't have happened. The problem was that I wanted it to happen again. Clearly Jun did too. I shook my head. "You are going to get yourself into so much trouble!" I scolded myself.

H3RO

Being so flustered with Jun, it wasn't until I was approaching the outer limits of Seoul that I even realized what I was wearing. I was still in my summer dress. Cute for the beach, but not really work appropriate. To be fair, the meeting was unscheduled, but had my thoughts been focused, I would have had the sense to change. "See, this is why you cannot get involved with Jun," I muttered under my breath as I approached Sejin's office. "You can't even think straight."

Inhye gave me a nervous smile as I approached. "He's expecting you," she told me.

"Great, because I wasn't expecting him," I grumbled. "Do you have any idea what this is about?" I asked.

She shook her head. "He's angry though, be careful."

"Don't worry—if it's about the retreat, I won't mention your name," I promised her. With that, I walked into the office, keeping my head held high. "Lee Sejin, I have six weeks left to make this album. I don't appreciate being made to drop everything to come see you."

"It took you three hours to get here. I don't see what exactly it was you dropped!" Sejin snapped at me.

I tilted my head. That meant he didn't know where I was, which meant he didn't know where H3RO was either. He had no idea about the cabin! "I am trying to make an album," I pointed out. "Which I'd like to get back to doing."

Lee Sejin clutched the edge of the table, his expression dark. "Is there a reason why you're not using honorifics with me?"

My eyes widened. "Is *that* what you dragged my ass over here for? And how have you only just noticed? I've been speaking like this to you for months."

"I am your *older* brother, as well as your employer. You should show me some respect!" he spat.

"Technically, our father is my employer," I told him, thankful for the first time for being able to use that word. "And I'm treating you with the respect you deserve, which, currently, is fuck all. Where I'm from, respect isn't automatically granted because of status. It's how you treat other people, *oppa*." I sneered as I rolled my eyes.

"You are not my sister," Sejin said, his voice turning acidic.

"Great!" I said with false cheer. "That rules out *oppa*. And seeing how that clears up everything, I'm going." I turned on my heel.

"Why did a KpopKonneKt go live with a campaign for H3RO today?"

I stopped and sucked in a breath in surprise. *That* was what he was upset about. I turned back to him and arched an eyebrow. Fifty dollars said it was because he thought it would reflect badly on Atlantis, rather than because he was actually ashamed of how H3RO had been treated. "Because you gave us zero budget, and I have to produce an album somehow."

"Do you have any idea how this is effecting the reputation of Atlantis Entertainment?" he demanded.

Bingo.

Sometimes it sucked to be right.

"Has it?" I asked. "Because so far, I've only seen a small blip of excitement about H3RO's comeback after a twenty-month absence," I said, pointedly. "Nothing about Atlantis' unfair treatment of one of their groups."

"It is business!" Sejin snarled, slamming his hand on his desk.

I arched an eyebrow at him for that. "So was starting a KpopKonneKt campaign. I had to be resourceful, and I found a way to raise those funds you were so adamant Atlantis couldn't afford. The good news is that everything the guys make will be profit."

"This album will make Atlantis the laughing stock

of the industry!"

"This KpopKonneKt campaign is going to make damn sure the exact opposite happens," I corrected him. "Did it ever occur to you, when you blocked every avenue to a songwriter, producer, and recording time; that releasing a flop will only make Atlantis look bad?!" I'd had enough. Sejin started ranting on about Atlantis Entertainment's reputation and I tuned out. I didn't even stick around, instead leaving his office.

I could hear him yelling behind the closed door, but I didn't go back in. Instead I was distracted by the good-looking guy—who had to be one of the actors or idols under the Atlantis label—standing in front of me. "It's true then," he said.

"What is?" I asked.

"H3RO is finally getting a comeback?"

Youngbin: that was his name. The leader and vocalist of Onyx—the much newer, yet much, much more successful group signed to Atlantis. He was several inches taller than me, with a long face and expressive eyes. "Only a year too late," I agreed.

"You're Lee Seungjin's sister, aren't you," he said, cocking his head and giving me a good once over.

I held my head high, wondering why my heart was pounding so much. Did it really matter if anyone knew who I was? I winced. Lee Sejin might not have wanted the company to know who I was, and until I started managing H3RO, I didn't care. Now, it was more that I didn't want them, H3RO, to find out. Not this way, at least.

As though he could hear my panicked thoughts, Youngbin held his hands up. "Seungjin said no one was to know, I'm sorry." He frowned. "I've been speaking to him a lot. He's going through a tough time right now, what with the scandal Bright Boys are caught up in."

I chewed at my lip, awkwardly. As well as Lee Sejin, I had another half-brother; Lee Seungjin. Seungjin was a member of Bright Boys, the group which, as Youngbin had said, were also struggling through a challenging time because of Atlantis. This was the group whose leader was supposedly caught up in a scandal which might have him forced to enlist early. I would have to check up on those guys later because, given how H3RO was being treated, I wasn't completely convinced the rumors about them were true. "I don't really know Seungjin," I admitted. "I didn't know I had a family out here until recently."

Youngbin glanced at the closed office door behind me and frowned. "Seungjin is a decent kid. He could do with someone in his family who isn't a complete dick."

"You think that's me?" I asked, surprised.

"You're the first one to really fight for H3RO. We all thought they would be disbanded, and yet here they are having a comeback," Youngbin shrugged. "You can't be all bad."

I grinned. "You sure you're not just saying that because I'm the boss?"

"Oh, I'm definitely saying it because you're the boss, but equally, I wouldn't say it if I didn't think it was true."

Strangely, his words touched me. It was nice to hear someone say I was doing something right. "This might be an appropriate time to ask a favor of you then," I said, another idea suddenly springing to mind.

"OK …?" Youngbin responded, sounding

hesitant.

I held my hands up. "No tricks," I promised him. "And no need for commitment if it's not something you're comfortable with, but I'm starting H3RO's SNS up again." I scowled. "I'm giving them SNS," I corrected myself. Something that earned me a wry scoff from Youngbin. "Would you mind sharing their accounts? I'm not trying to steal your fan-base, and honestly, I don't think your Black Gems are going anywhere, even if I paid them, but it would be good for a little publicity."

"Oh, is that all?" Youngbin exclaimed, looking relieved. "Of course, I can do that. I'll get the rest of Onyx to do it as well. We've always been rooting for our *sunbaes.*"

I breathed out a sigh of relief and fixed him a grateful smile. "Thank you."

"Sure," he nodded. Then he pulled out his phone. "Let's exchange numbers and if you think of anything else we can do, just give me a call."

I pulled out my phone and swapped with Youngbin, quickly typing in my number. As I took mine back, another thought hit me. "Can I ask another favor?"

"Of course," Youngbin agreed.

"That asshole in there hates me and wants nothing to do with me. In some respects, I don't blame him," I sighed. I was the illegitimate child coming to potentially take a place in a company I'm sure he assumed was going to be all his. "I've not spoken to Seungjin. I'm not even sure he wants to meet me … would you pass on my number and give him the option? I mean, if he's not interested, I won't force it. I just think

I would like to try with him."

"Sure," Youngbin nodded with a genuine smile.

We parted ways and I headed back to the elevator. Just as the door was shutting, a blur entered with me. "Inhye, we have to stop meeting like this!" I exclaimed.

"You went to KpopKonneKt," she said.

I nodded, wondering where she was taking this.

"I overheard the conversation," she continued. "Lee Sejin isn't quiet. I want to help."

I gave her an appreciative smile but shook my head. "I don't want you to get in trouble with Sejin."

"I have a brother-in-law who is a hair stylist. He opened his salon recently, so it's not that famous, but he's good. He's also willing to do it at a lower cost than normal trade price, provided you're happy to bring H3RO in after hours." Once again, a folded piece of paper was thrust into my hand as the door opened, then Inhye darted out before I could thank her.

This place was exhausting.

Before leaving, I made my way to the tech department. It took some convincing, but I managed to leave with a laptop and a brand-new iPad. Then I was on my way to the airport, it was time to pick up Kate.

제8 장

H3RⲈ

You Are

Kyun, Nate, and Jun were waiting for us when we got back. "Minhyuk hasn't left the studio," Nate complained. "I'm starving."

"It's good to see you too," I retorted. "This is Kate, by the way."

Kate gave the guys a finger wave. "S'up?"

Kate was one of these girls who looked effortlessly gorgeous. She had shoulder-length auburn hair, though it was currently tied back in a bun, and sharp, dark eyes, that were highlighted by her mad skills with an eyeliner—even after a fourteen-hour flight. She was also about four inches taller than me, with a killer figure.

Kate pulled her sunglasses up as she leaned into me. "Dude, you could have warned me they were all hot. I look like crap," she hissed at me in English.

"You look like you stepped off a runway," I told her, marginally annoyed that she did. I'd gone puffy after my flight. "And the middle one is Nate. He's from San Francisco. He can understand us."

Nate winked at her. Smooth as anything, Kate dropped her sunglasses back down and smiled at him. "Well I wasn't lying. You're fine as fuck, dude."

I quickly introduced her to Kyun and Jun, and then led her upstairs to my bedroom. "This one is all yours," I told her.

"Holly," she hissed at me. "I know you think the Korean side of your family are dicks, but you're not doing too badly out here. Those three are Grade A hotties, and Nate definitely has a thing for you."

"Nate?" I repeated. "*Nate?*" I was expecting her to say Jun, if anything (although I was glad she hadn't picked up on that one).

"He was the American one, right?" When I nodded, she wiggled her eyebrows at me. "The guy couldn't take his eyes off you."

"I think you're jet-lagged," I laughed.

"I think you're in denial, but whatever," she shrugged, finally looking around the room. "Sweet digs, Holls."

"It's the company retreat," I explained. "The dorms are a lot smaller and more basic than this. I'm going to order pizza. Settle in and have a nap if you need to. I'll call you down when it's here."

I went back downstairs to the kitchen, leaning on the top of the kitchen island as I scrolled through my phone, trying to find a local pizza delivery service. "I'm ordering pizza," I announced. "What does everyone want?"

Jun got up from the table, walking around the island to join me. As he passed me, he squeezed my butt. I jumped in the air, my phone clattering to the counter top, causing both Nate and Kyun to look over.

I turned to glower at Jun, but he calmly scooped up my phone and examined the screen like nothing had happened. "Done," he said, turning so his back was to the others. As he handed it over to me, he smirked, then sauntered back to the table to join them.

"Just pepperoni for me," Nate called.

"Kyun?"

"I'll have ramyun," he muttered.

Weirdo. I wandered out to the studio, taking my phone with me. The remaining three guys were in one of the rooms at the back. It held a keyboard and a few guitars, which thankfully Tae had been able to tune.

Minhyuk was in the corner, facing the wall. It looked like he was silently rapping. Every so often he would pause and scribble something down. Dante was gently playing a melody on the keyboard, while Tae seemed to be transcribing it onto paper. The last time I had been in here, they had all been staring at a different wall, so this seemed like progress.

When they hadn't realized I was standing there after a few minutes, I gently tapped on the door. Three heads swung around to stare at me. "I'm ordering pizza," I said.

Minhyuk's eyes went wide. "Is it dinner time already?"

"You must have been having a productive day," I smiled.

"It would be easier if we could put it straight into a music program," Tae shrugged.

"Is that something like Cube-base?" I asked, trying to remember what the software was that the tech had been insistent I have.

"Cubase, yeah, why?" Tae asked.

"Well, I don't know what else you need, seeing as you said half your equipment is missing out here, but I have a laptop with Cubase on with me. Will that help?"

Minhyuk leaped around the keyboard and hugged me. As I glanced over his shoulder, for a moment, I thought Tae and Dante were going to do the same thing. "Boys and their toys," I muttered in amusement as Minhyuk pulled away.

"I'm sorry I forgot about dinner," he said.

"Why?" I asked. "It's not like you have to cook every night. Besides, when you guys get around to giving me your order, we're having pizza anyway."

"Cooking is Minhyuk's chore," Tae shrugged as I tossed the phone to him.

"It's not really a chore if you enjoy it," Minhyuk told me.

I gave the three a look of surprise. "You guys all have chores?"

"Yes, otherwise we would live in a pigsty," Tae replied as he handed the phone to Dante.

"Unless you're Jun, and then you avoid them at all costs," Minhyuk added.

"You're too easy on him," Tae scolded Minhyuk, good naturedly. "You let him get away with not washing the dishes all the time."

The phone made its way back to me and I submitted the order. "You have twenty minutes and you're not getting the laptop until after dinner."

H3RO

At some point during dinner, although I told her it wasn't necessary, Kate started working. I made sure to stay out of the way, watching from a distance as I finished putting the finishing touches to the various SNS accounts. Instagram, Twitter, and Facebook were live. I'd had to access the Atlantis network to find the passwords, then spent hours archiving junk off them. There hadn't been that much posted to start with, but there were a lot of shares and reposts which had nothing to do with H3RO. Apparently, Hanjoo had been using it for his own benefit. I had finally worked out how to create a fancafe, which was ready to go when we hit 50,000 followers on Instagram. I was just waiting for the approval for the V Live, but I also wanted some recent shots for that.

After a while, Kate handed me a memory card. "Have fun with that," she told me. There was a wicked grin on her face, and I couldn't wait to see what she had managed to catch. For someone with such an outgoing personality, she had the ability to hide in the background. She'd always managed to take great shots, even at college. I'd also seen a few of the US pop star's tour photographs, and they were amazing.

I sat flicking through the photographs and settled on a few of the first ones. It was a candid shot of the six guys sat at the table, passing the pizza around.

[헤로] 피자로 우리의 첫 게시물을 축하합니다! Celebrating our first post with pizza! ☐ **#H3RO #태 #단테 #네이트 #민혁 #균 #준 #피자 #우리가당신의영웅이되어주세요**

I wasn't the best at marketing, but for the first post, it was enough. I hit post, making sure to cross-post it to Twitter and Facebook.

No sooner had I set the iPad down, it went crazy. Notification after notification came through. Oops. I had forgotten to turn those off. By the time I had gone through the settings and refreshed the home screen, we'd already gained eighteen thousand followers on Instagram. Buried in there were several reposts from Onyx members. Youngbin's comment made me laugh: **Do I smell pizza, or a comeback? Guess I'm gunna have to follow to find out.**

I made the mistake of getting lost in the blackhole of Instagram, liking comments, following back a surprising number of other idols who had followed us.

"May we have that laptop?"

I pulled myself away and found Tae, Dante and Minhyuk watching me, twitching excitedly. "Huh? Oh, yes, of course!" I quickly collected it and handed it over. Then I relocated myself to the couch and continued into my black hole of SNS.

The fancafe went live three hours later.

Somewhere in between then, I let Jun free with the second iPad. My own iPad was slowly being spammed with notifications of H3RO going live. At that point, I switched my own notifications off and got back to work. I was trying to come up with the comeback schedule, which was hard enough when there still wasn't a definitive date.

It was Nate waving a bottle of water in front of my face which broke me free of my work and I looked up at him with blurry eyes. "You kinda look like crap," he told me.

"And I just found out who the charmer is in the group," I yawned, rubbing at my face.

"Go get some sleep," he instructed me. "It's three

in the morning."

I yawned again and looked at the clock on my iPad. It was. My iPad battery was also dying, and Kate had gone to bed hours ago, inconveniently where my charger was. "I plan on sleeping here," I shrugged. "I'm waiting for you guys to go to bed."

Nate snorted. "You gave Jun an iPad. He's not going to sleep tonight."

I groaned, raking my hands through my hair. "He'll pass out eventually," I yawned.

"Look at him," Nate disagreed, shaking his head at me. "He's like that Energizer bunny. He's going to be going for hours."

"Probably."

"You also gave Tae the ability to lay some tracks down. He, Dante and Minhyuk won't be going to bed tonight either. Go take one of their rooms."

"Not going to offer up your own bed then?" I teased him.

"You are more than welcome to get into my bed, but I plan on going to sleep soon myself," he said, his eyes smoldering down at me.

Wow, I needed some sleep. Jun let out a boisterous cheer and I made my decision. "I'm stealing Minhyuk's bed," I announced. It was likely to be the cleanest.

Wearily, I headed up to bed. In his bedroom, I let out a sigh: I hadn't taken my things from my room before Kate had gone to bed. Oh well. I pulled open a drawer, grabbed a T-shirt and replaced my dress with it. It was long and smelled reassuringly familiar. As an afterthought, I grabbed a Post-It from my bag and scrawled a quick note—*I stole your bed. Holly*—and stuck it on the bedroom door. Just in case. Then I crawled into bed.

When I woke up again, it felt like hours had passed. I picked my phone up, squinting at the brightness of the screen and discovered it had been less than half an hour. I dropped the phone, groaning as I rolled over.

And found a pair of eyes glinting at me in the dim light coming from the lock screen of my phone.

"Holy shit!" I squealed, performing an act that was a weird cross between a scuttle and a leap backwards. I fell out of the bed tangled up in a web of bedsheets. "Fuck a duck!" I grunted, rubbing at the elbow I had smacked on a bedside cabinet on the way down. Thankfully, it was a low bed.

"I'd rather you left the poultry alone," Nate said, pulling a face as he appeared above me, hanging over the side of the bed. "If you're feeling horny, I know someone who could help with that."

"What are you doing in Minhyuk's bed?" I demanded as I tried to extract myself from the knot I'd managed to get into. I'd succeeded in freeing one arm and a leg. The other was under my back and I couldn't pull it free.

Nate tilted his head. "Minhyuk's bed? Holly, you're in my bed."

"No, I'm in Minhyuk's," I corrected him, then let out a grunt as I collapsed back onto the floor. I was stuck. "I even put a Post-It on the door."

"Yeah, my door," Nate pointed out. "I figured you'd changed your mind about sharing." He tilted his head in the other direction. "Do you need some help?"

"I was wondering when you were going to

notice," I grumbled. "Yes, please. I'm stuck."

Nate dropped off the bed and crouched down beside me. "What have you done?" he laughed, trying to pull a corner free.

"You scared me out of my bed," I snapped, the embarrassment finally setting in.

"My bed," Nate corrected me. He shifted his weight, and then he was kneeling beside me.

I could feel my heart speed up, so I bit my lip, trying to calm myself down. Then Nate's hand brushed up my leg and I let out a small squeal.

"Sorry," Nate mumbled. He tugged at something, and then I felt the blankets slacken off enough for me to wriggle free.

I sat upright, and promptly headbutted Nate. "Sorry," I quickly apologized in horror. Nate winced in pain. "Where did I hit you? Are you OK?" I peered at him, bringing my head in close, though slowly, trying to make out in the near darkness if he was bleeding. At the same time, Nate turned his head to face me, and then there was a hair's breadth between us.

For an unknown length of time, neither of us moved, both of us barely breathing. "I think it needs kissing better," Nate suddenly whispered.

"Where?" I wasn't sure if I said it aloud, or if I had imagined myself saying it.

Then Nate responded in another whisper. "My lips."

I stared at him, blinking, and then burst out laughing. I laughed so hard, I ended up doubled over with tears streaming down my cheeks. "Your lips?" I repeated amidst a snort. Beside me, slowly, Nate started to join in. "My sides hurt," I gasped.

"You want me to kiss them better?" Nate offered, setting us back off into peals of laughter again.

"That was terrible," I groaned when the laugher had finally subsided. We were lying on our backs, side by side, staring up at the ceiling.

"I'm normally smoother than that," Nate protested.

"I'm adding 'No good at chat-up lines' to your bio," I told him, shaking my head in amusement.

Beside me, Nate stood. Upright, he leaned over and offered me a hand. I took it and he pulled me to my feet. Somehow, the movement had me toe to toe with him. Before I could step back, an arm shot around my waist, drawing me flush against his body.

I looked up and found him staring down at me with a look that said he couldn't work out what he wanted to do next.

May the K-Pop gods help me, I made the decision for him.

I stood on my toes, and the distance between us evaporated. The grip around me tightened, and my lips met his.

It was gentle. Despite the fact his arm was wrapped around me, I couldn't stop the doubt that shot through me. Slowly, I started to move my lips against his.

There was no hesitation from Nate as he returned the kiss. As I relaxed into him, I became aware that the T-shirt I was wearing was doing little to keep the heat of his hard chest from me, his tongue teased at my lips. I parted them and his tongue slid in my mouth, staking it's claim.

My hands, which until now had been resting on

his shoulder blades, slid up and around his neck, like I needed to hold him in place. Like he knew what I wanted, he titled his head, his tongue making long, lazy strokes over mine, again and again.

Eventually, far too soon, he pulled away, breathing heavily as he rested his forehead against mine. "I'm taking that as payment for you stealing my bed," he said in a throaty whisper. He pressed his lips against mine one last time, and before I had worked out what he was doing, he had left me alone in the room.

I turned, dropping heavily on the bed, and flopped backwards, placing the back of my hands on my cheeks, in a poor attempt to cool them. Jun and now Nate? What the hell was wrong with me?

제 9 장

H3R오

Irresistible Lips

The guilt was firmly set in place when I emerged from Nate's bedroom after a restless few hours of sleep. I was supposed to be managing these guys, not making out with them ... or more than that, in Jun's case.

Kate was already up and dressed when I left Nate's room, so I got showered and picked out my clothes in her room. "No more fooling around with idols," I scolded my reflection after I had finished brushing my teeth. "You have a job to do."

When I felt I had sufficiently reprimanded myself and made the decision to ignore anything vaguely flirt-worthy, I went downstairs. The kitchen was already full. Minhyuk had emerged from the studio to cook breakfast, assisted by Kyun. Behind them, perched at the island, were Dante and Tae. Over the top of the kitchen activity, they seemed to be bouncing ideas off each other.

I glanced over to the dining table and my heart leapt into my throat. Kate was sitting with Jun and Nate.

It took me ten precious seconds to realize the camera Jun had claimed was between them and judging from how Jun and Kate kept looking to Nate, he was translating the conversation between them.

Not feeling ready to join in that conversation, I slid onto the stool next to Dante. "Sounds like you guys have had a productive night." I peered at his face. "Why do I feel like none of you have managed to get any sleep?"

"We haven't," Dante agreed.

Minhyuk turned around, serving the side dishes and handing them over to Dante who carried them over to the table. "Once we had our hands on Cubase, we accomplished a lot," he explained as he worked. "We've gotten two tracks down."

"You have?" I asked, surprised, but pleased. "That's brilliant news!"

"Don't get too excited," Tae muttered. "They're samples. We still need to get into a studio and record. Then they really need a producer working on them, because I'm not good enough for that."

"I think what you've done and what you're still doing is great," Minhyuk assured him.

"Great for a sample, but nowhere near good enough for what it needs to be for release," he grumbled. He sounded dejected at that, but before I could say anything, he had picked up some more items and taken them to the table.

"Y'all know it's breakfast, right?" I heard Kate exclaim as she looked at the amount of food on the table.

"Korean breakfast," I called over to her. "You get used to it."

She got up and walked over. "Any chance of a bowl of Lucky Charms?"

I pointed at the fruit bowl and she pulled a face. "Dude, it's too early to be eating that much food. And rice for breakfast?"

"You majored in Japanese," I pointed out.

"And?"

"You lived there for a year."

"And?" I gave her a pointed look. "I still managed to eat Lucky Charms."

"You majored in Japanese?" Nate repeated as he joined my other side.

The hair on my arms shot up like there was suddenly a charge in the air. I kept my attention on Minhyuk, willing him to hurry up so I had an excuse to walk to the table and away from Nate. This would not do at all.

Kate nodded. "I lived in a small town outside of Tokyo for a year. It wasn't too bad in the city, but where I was, there weren't that many people who spoke English. I came back much more proficient. It trips me up sometimes, but I'm almost fluent in it now."

"Guys, she speaks Japanese," he declared, loudly, in Korean.

"You guys speak Japanese?" I asked him, before I could remember I was trying to ignore him. My eyes went wide, and I quickly looked back to Minhyuk. Seriously, how long did it take to spoon out kimchi?

"We did a couple of Japanese albums early on," Nate explained. I could see him giving me an odd look from the corner of my eye. "Kyun and Minhyuk are nearly fluent themselves. The rest of us know bits. Probably more than she knows of Korean."

Beside me, Kate was getting excited. Before I knew it, she was babbling with Minhyuk in what I could only assume was Japanese.

I didn't speak a word of it. Kate and I knew each other because we had shared the bathroom between our dorm rooms, not because we had the same majors. Finally, Minhyuk passed the kimchi over, and I snatched it up before Dante, who had returned for more.

Being at the table now presented me with another problem: Jun. He looked up, caught my eye, and when I felt my face begin to heat up, gave me that smirk. I gritted my teeth and sat down … at the opposite end of the table. I pulled out my phone in an attempt to look busy. I kept my eyes firmly locked on it until all the food had been placed on the table, and everyone was seated. I was tempted to stay on it, but my mom would have had a fit if I had. Instead, I focused on the food.

"Holly is staying in my room," Nate suddenly announced.

I started choking on my beansprouts.

"Kate has taken her room. I'll share with Jun," he continued as Kate thumped at my back, giving me a look which said she was thoroughly entertained at my discomfort. "Just thought I should let you know in case any of you decide to wander in there naked … Jun I'm talking about you."

I looked up and ended up catching Jun's eye. His eyebrows had completely disappeared under his hair. "I thought it was Dante I had to watch out for. I didn't realize you liked to let it all hang free too."

Beside me, Kate paused in eating. "What did you say?!" she hissed at me, irritated and frustrated at the Korean conversation. "Why are you turning pink?

What's going on?"

"You watch out for me?" Dante asked, grinning.

I pulled a face at him. "I'm not responding to that."

"So, that's a yes!"

I rolled my eyes. "That's an, 'I'm eating, and I don't want to be put off my food'."

"I think you like me," he taunted.

"Don't you have an album to finish?" I shot at him.

Dante laughed, getting up from the table. Without responding, but still grinning, he disappeared out towards the studio. Shaking his head, Tae followed. I forced myself to remain cool and collected. Or at least as cool and collected as I could, which probably wasn't very much, and finished what was left of my breakfast. Only then did I make my excuses and head to the couch to collect the iPad from where I had left it again this morning when I had finally been able to put it on charge.

Kate hurried after me, sitting down beside me. "Dude?!"

"Dude," I returned.

"Don't dude me," she retorted. "Have I been reading this wrong all this time? Is it Dante? Are you hooking up with him?"

I lowered my iPad with a sigh, though I was silently thanking the gods that she had gone for Dante. "No, I am not hooking up with Dante. Get that idea out of your head."

"Pfft," she muttered. "Maybe you should put that idea in *your* head. That guy is fine as fuck. If he starts flirting with me, I can't promise you I'm not gonna flirt back, unless you tell me now he's off limits."

My eyes narrowed. "Hang on a minute, that whole conversation was in Korean."

"I learned Korean overnight," she said, deadpan. When I arched an eyebrow at her, she shrugged. "I spent a year in Japan where I knew next to no Japanese. I had to get by on body language for a long time. Judging from the way he was trying to undress you with his eyes, I would say he totally wants you." She frowned. "To be fair, I'm fairly certain Nate and Jun have a thing for you too." She half swiveled in her seat to be able to look over her shoulder at Nate and Jun who were busy cleaning the table, thankfully meaning I didn't have to look her in the eye. "Not gonna lie, dude, I wouldn't turn any of them down."

She turned back to me and I sighed. "Well I'd be lying if I said they weren't all hot."

"Yeah you would," she agreed.

"You might want to wipe that drool away," I sniped.

Kate shrugged, dropping back into the couch. "Turns out I have a type. Hot Asian guys."

I laughed and picked the iPad back up. "Why don't you go take photos of them then. Make them look good for me.

"Holly, they do that all by themselves. They don't need any help from me."

No. No, they didn't.

Mentally shaking myself, I dove back into work.

H3RO

Nothing was mentioned by either Jun or Nate about the

conversation at breakfast. For the most part, I was left alone to get on with work. At some point in the middle of the afternoon, Nate appeared to push a couple of kimbap triangles my way.

In the evening, I was dragged back to the table for more pizza. With Minhyuk still in the studio, and apparently no one else with the ability to cook, pizza had been their solution. I would have to pay more attention, because we didn't have the money to be spending this much on food, especially not when we had stocked up with so many groceries.

After so little sleep the night before, I ended up retiring for the night quite early. This time I had remembered to move my things to Nate's room. I had just finished brushing my teeth when there was a soft rap at the door. I padded over and opened it, finding Nate there.

"Forget something?" I asked, stepping back to let him in.

Nate walked in, shutting the door behind him. "I'm here for my payment."

I looked up at him, wrinkling my nose up in confusion. "Huh?"

His response was to kiss me. When his hands slid around me, pulling my body up against his, I gasped. He took advantage of that, deepening the kiss. And, so help me, I kissed him back. Once again, his kisses were slow, his tongue almost massaging mine. It was like some beautiful torture, but I couldn't stop myself.

Like the night before, it was Nate who broke away first. "Payment collected."

I blinked up at him, trying to see him through the haze of lust which had set in. "Huh?" Words, it seemed, had escaped me. He stepped back away from me, his hand resting on the door handled. "Holly, don't act weird with me," he said, before stepping out of the door.

Holy hell, I was screwed.

제10 장

H3RO

Come Back When You Hear This Song

The rest of the time at the retreat seemed to play on repeat. I would be working for maybe sixteen hours of the day. Most of that time was spent emailing or calling various people to try to book things for H3RO. I had a suspicion that Sejin was blacklisting us, but I had absolutely no proof of it, and no one I could speak to about it.

I was getting worried too. Tae had been saying this morning that they were almost ready to head back to the dorms and get the tracks recorded and polished. Only I had nowhere for them to do that.

That wasn't quite true. There was a place in Busan that could take us, but it would eat up most of the KpopKonneKt budget. Not that it would help us.

Financially, we were good. Within the week, we had broken the 100% goal and were currently hovering around 300%. But I was also finding it impossible to find anyone who was free to shoot the music video. Somehow *everyone* in South Korea was "busy". I was at the point where I was trying to get in contact with some

US video directors. I'd found a few, but they weren't cheap.

Aside from the fact I was close to having a major stress out, the guys seemed to be in great spirits. Tae, Dante and Minhyuk spent most of the time in the studio, though they weren't ready to share anything yet, and Kyun, Nate and Jun were taking control of the social media accounts.

And Kate was successfully getting all of it on film.

We had one last night in the retreat before returning to Seoul. Kate was going to stick around for a few more weeks. I had already promised her the keys to my unused apartment, along with the Range Rover for her to explore when we were stuck in the dorm (although she had declined the latter, saying she couldn't read street signs so she probably shouldn't be driving— I was inclined to agree). I had called Inhye's brother-in-law and he had excitedly booked us in, promising that a night next week was all ours.

That was also causing me stress, even mixed in with the relief. Because what the hell concept were we going with? What was the music video going to be? Hell, what was the song? I wasn't even sure all this was being done in the right order. I'd had a plan: song, makeover, music video. I'd hoped to stick to it. Yet everything and everyone seemed to be doing their best to stop it. I was once again, seriously doubting if I was cut out for this.

I wish I could have said that was the end of my stress. But H3RO themselves were adding to it. Or, half of them, at least. My biggest worry was with Kyun. He was by no means overweight, but in the last two weeks he had lost weight. He was spending a lot of time in the gym, and more worryingly, he wasn't eating anywhere near as much as the others.

I fully understood that a huge part of being an idol was caught up in his appearance, but he really didn't have to worry. When I'd asked him about it, he promised me—albeit quite sharply—that he was eating small, regular meals, and that his only aim was that he wanted to find his abs. He'd gotten moody and defensive and walked off.

Then there was Nate. I was still sleeping in his bed, and every night he was still coming to collect his 'payment'. And damnit, I would look forward to those toe-curling kisses. I shouldn't have been. I was fully aware that what was happening should not have been. But he always left me craving more. He had never tried to take it beyond a kiss. I'd really had to fight myself to not take the lead on that. As it was, kisses could just about be excused.

He would continue to bring me snacks and drinks, and outside of that bedroom you would never have been able to tell that anything had happened between us. Yet, even though the guilt was churning my insides up, I couldn't stop myself from kissing him.

Jun, on the other hand, was a walking smirk. He would continue to brush up against me, seemingly innocently in front of the others, but his hand would linger on my butt or legs just a little too long. Every so often he would fix me a look—no, not just a look ... it was a silent message. There were no words, but there didn't need to be. It was getting to a point where I didn't trust myself to be alone with this maknae.

The doorbell rang and I frowned before hurrying to answer the door. At first, I was surprised when I saw a delivery guy with trays crammed full of sushi, piled high in his arms. Then I was dismayed. This wouldn't have been cheap and at this point, every won counted.

Then Kate bounded past me with her card. "Nate told me I could pay these guys with a card! Dude, you should have said something sooner!"

I took half of the trays and helped her carry them through. Everyone was already waiting outside, and five sets of eyes lit up when they saw the amount of food we were carrying.

Five ... that wasn't right. I quickly scanned the area. "Where's Dante?" I asked, expecting it to be Kyun that was missing.

"Finishing up in the studio," Minhyuk muttered, though his attention was fixed firmly on the sushi.

I set the trays down with a sigh. If Dante didn't appear soon, he wasn't going to get any. I grabbed a tray before anyone noticed and took it back into the kitchen—just in case. Then I continued through to the studio. "Dante?" I called from the door. I could hear running water from the back and assumed he was getting a drink from the small kitchen in there. "Dante?" I called again.

A door opened and Dante walked out.

Naked.

Again.

My mouth dropped open, but I couldn't look away. Once again, Dante stared me down, his arms folded, and an eyebrow cocked. Ah, hell, that was not the right word to be using in this situation ...

He was soaking wet, like he'd just stepped out of a shower—I didn't even know there was a shower back here—and drops of water were dripping from his hair. I watched one droplet as it ran down his neck, down his chest, and down the curling tail of his tattoo towards ... my eyes shot up and I found Dante smirking at me. "Like what you see?"

"Why the hell aren't you wearing clothes?" I demanded, my voice loud and shrieking because of my embarrassment.

"I just got out of the shower."

"Polite people wrap up in towels."

"Polite people don't stare," he retorted with a grin.

"Will you ... just ... wrap it up?" I spluttered.

The grin widened.

Unable to form any more words that weren't going to get him grinning smugly at me, I turned on my heel. "There's sushi in the house," I yelled over my shoulder as I bolted out of the studio.

Seriously? Who in the hell didn't dry off when they got out of the shower?

I returned to the poolside, grateful that I could distract myself with food. I was also grateful I had taken a tray inside because there was very little remaining outside. I was about to head in and grab it when Nate slid a plate under my nose, offering me a pair of chopsticks. "Thank you," I muttered, sinking back down.

He sat down next to me, watching me eat. "You've lost weight," he told me. "You're not looking after yourself."

I didn't comment. He was right. I had noticed that my clothes were getting looser, but that was because I was so caught up in work that I was losing track of time. It wasn't intentional.

"Looks like I'm going to have to look after you

better," he said.

I had a mouth full of a roll, so all I could do was narrow my eyes at him. He simply laughed and walked away. By the time I had managed to chew and swallow, he was at the other end of the pool with Minhyuk.

Dante came out soon after that, thankfully now fully clothed, carrying the spare tray of sushi. He set it down on the table in front of me, and although I tried to keep my focus on my plate, when he didn't move, I couldn't help but look up. "You need something else to put in your mouth?" he asked me.

I stared up at him, my eyes wide.

"What is he saying to you?" Kate asked, suddenly appearing beside me. She looked between the two of us.

I ignored her. "I'll let you know when I see something I like."

"Oh, baby," he sighed, tutting. "I've already seen that hunger. You let me know when you're ready to feast."

Damnit, he was annoyingly arrogant. And annoyingly right.

I also had no witty comeback for him.

"Seriously, can you just drag him to your bed, already?" Kate asked, rolling her eyes.

"I am his manager," I told her. That phrase was becoming my mantra.

"So, quit. Problem solved."

I had no chance to respond because Tae was suddenly standing beside me. "Or him," Kate muttered in my ear. "Because if you don't, I really will."

I ignored her, and the sudden flash of jealousy that appeared, and instead looked up at H3RO's leader. "Hi, Tae."

"Do you have some time?"

"Of course," I said. "Is everything OK?"

"Look, they're only rough and far from the finished thing, so don't be too disappointed, but we're ready to let everyone listen to the demos," Tae explained, awkwardly rubbing at the back of his neck.

"Yes!" I exclaimed loudly, drawing the attention of everyone with my excitement. I didn't care. I jumped to my feet. "Lead the way."

"Try not to get too excited," Tae mumbled. "You'll only end up disappointed."

"I highly doubt that!" I scoffed. I pulled Kate up beside me. "Sorry, friend, but you're back on work duty. I want photographs to record this momentous occasion."

Tae stopped, turning back to me so suddenly that I only just avoided walking into him. "This doesn't require photographs," he growled at me.

I held my hands up and stepped back. "OK, no photos." Inside I was seething. I was absolutely convinced beyond all doubt that the three of them would have pulled something together. The fact that his doubt was so imprinted in him had me wanting to drive back to Seoul. I had no idea exactly what had been said to him over the years by Sejin, but I really wanted to punch him. I also wanted to wrap my arms around Tae. "Change of plan," I told Kate.

"It's cool," she said, sitting back down. "You go deal with that. I'll go pack."

Tae had already walked off, so I followed behind. Dante fell into step beside me. "He's worked hard on this."

"You all have," I told him. "I'm convinced you're

all running off fumes, and I'm sure you've managed to have less sleep than me." The others were already waiting in the studio when Dante and I arrived. I took a seat on one of the couches beside Jun and Minhyuk and waited patiently for Tae.

"You've all got to remember that it's not finished. We normally get our demos in a more developed stage than this, so don't expect too much," Tae started to explain.

"Ah, just play it, hyung," Nate told him. "We trust you."

I glanced around at Kyun and Jun. They hadn't really had much to do with the creating side of things, but they looked just as confident and trusting of the others as I did, and I could feel my heart melting.

Tae turned to face the laptop. He turned the speakers up and hit play.

I closed my eyes and let the music wash over me. I wasn't an expert. I had no experience when it came to producing music. I really had to work to try to envisage how Tae had wanted this to turn out considering he was so adamant it wasn't up to scratch ... but I liked it.

The second was a ballad. Ballads weren't really my thing, but then Dante started hitting high notes, and holy hell, it was a rough demo, but I got goosebumps.

But nothing prepared me for the third song. The opening bars had my heart racing. It was ... dangerous. "This one," I said, before I could stop myself. "This is your title track." I was no choreographer, but I had visions of them dancing to it. I was no cinematographer, but I could see the music video in my head too. The bass needed defining a little more, but it was mid-tempo, had a cracking beat, and it made me want to stick it on repeat.

"Are you sure?" Dante asked, uncertain.

I had no idea why he looked so unsure. "I already want to add this to my playlist," I informed them. "And for the record, Lee Sejin is an asshole who knows nothing about music."

"He's running Atlantis," Tae pointed out.

"Yeah, but it's his father's company," Jun said with a frown. "Lee Woojin was the one who created Atlantis Entertainment."

It was my turn to frown as I looked at Tae. "Wait. Did my …," I quickly caught myself. "Did Lee Woojin tell you that you had no talent too?"

Tae shook his head. "Lee Woojin has had little to do with our career. He picked us out during the audition, and I believe it was him who picked us out to debut in H3RO, but that's it."

That brought me a little comfort. I had a lot of anger towards Lee Woojin, but I really didn't want to add this to the list.

"What did you say it was called?" I asked them.

"It's 'Who Is Your Hero?'," Minhyuk replied.

I smiled. "Play it again for me."

Tae stared at me, his expression blank. "Don't you want to hear the other songs?"

"Absolutely!" I exclaimed. "But I need to hear this one more time first."

His mouth quirked up into the briefest of smiles as he turned to play the song again. I sat back and closed my eyes again. This time, I listened to the lyrics. I had been so absorbed by the melody and the beat the first time around, I had only caught the odd phrase. Halfway through, I realized this song wasn't a love song. This was a song about becoming the hero of your own story: facing down your demons, defeating your enemies; how you didn't need H3RO to be the hero because you already were one.

Forget title song, this was going to be the theme song to my life!

제11 장

H3RO

Tell Me What to Do

The serenity which had settled over me when I'd listened to the whole album lasted the night. The following day, on the way back to Seoul, the panic was back. H3RO had done their job. They had written six fantastic songs.

But I had yet to deliver them a recording studio. Or a producer.

The nine-seater minibus was cramped with the eight of us and all the luggage, but unlike the trip to the cabin, the atmosphere was much happier. I dropped Kate off outside my apartment block, promising I would be back for her in a few days' time for the album artwork.

We had barely arrived at the dorm before Tae, Dante and Minhyuk had gathered around me. "What?" I asked, warily.

"When do we get into the studio?" Minhyuk asked. He was like an excited child, hopping back and forth between each foot.

While their excitement warmed me, they couldn't

thaw out the chill that had me frozen at the lack of answer I held to that question. What studio? "Not today," I told him. "I wasn't sure what time we would be back." I pointed down the corridor to their rooms. "Go rest. You three have barely slept over the last few weeks. Turn your humidifiers on and sleep."

I was thankfully saved from further questioning by my phone bleeping at me. Annoyingly, it was a text message from Sejin. In just three words I could feel the hate he was sending me: **My office. Now.** What had I done to piss him off this time?

I gave the guys a smile and excused myself. "Work beckons," I muttered as I left the building.

As I was already so close to the Atlantis Entertainment office, I decided to walk. I had spent the day driving and I wasn't eager to get back in a minibus again. The streets were busy, especially outside the building. There were a lot of Onyx and Cupcake fans, eager for a glance of their beloved idols … and, I was happy to see, a couple of girls with signs expressing the love for H3RO. OK, it was small numbers, but it was two more than it had been the last time I was there! That was a massive improvement and I was taking that as a win.

Inside, I went straight to Sejin's office. This time, I waited for Inhye to say it was OK for me to go in. I had a sneaky suspicion Sejin would have reprimanded her the last time I had barged in, and that hadn't been her fault.

Sejin had the second largest office in the building. The biggest, I'd only been in once, belonged to his father; *our* father. With that being said, Sejin's office was still enormous, with two walls being made up entirely of outside facing windows. Instead of being seated behind his desk, Sejin was stood, staring out across the city, his arms clasped behind his back.

Looking at him, I was beginning to suspect my small stature was a gift from my mother's side of the family. Sejin was tall and lanky. He reminded me of a Western Coppermouth. I'd come across them occasionally back in Chicago, and I wasn't sure which was deadlier.

Sejin turned around and glided over to me. It was like watching a vampire from the old Hollywood movies. His hair was certainly slicked back in that style. "Would you care to explain why all my artists are promoting your waste of space group?"

"Atlantis Entertainments'," I corrected him.

"What?" he hissed.

"Would you care to explain why all of Atlantis Entertainments' artists are promoting one of Atlantis Entertainments' groups?" I said, slowly, enunciating each word. "They're not your idols. They're the company's."

Sejin took three steps closer, closing the gap between us. He towered over me, but I refused to step back. He wasn't going to intimidate me. "What?" he spat.

"You heard me," I shrugged.

"You have no idea what takes place in my company," he growled at me.

I pulled a face. "I *wish* I had no idea what took place in this company. And, the last I checked, you're still not in the biggest office."

"That's for appearances' only," Sejin told me. "Everyone knows I'm the one who holds the power here."

I stared at him, ready to comment, then shook my head. "I'm not arguing this one with you," I said with a shrug. I turned on my heel and made my way to the door.

"That's right. You leave. And keep walking, all the way to the exit."

I paused and glanced back. "Oh, I'll keep walking, but I'm heading to Lee Woojin's office. I'm going to find out exactly who is the one with the power."

The smug look fell from Sejin's face like a lead balloon. "Holly!" he bellowed.

I ignored him and marched down the corridors, politely smiling and nodding my head at the various people I passed. I was aware that Sejin was behind me, hurrying to catch up, but equally trying not to make a scene. I kept my pace brisk. I didn't stop longer than to tap at Lee Woojin's door before ignoring his secretary and walking in.

Woojin wasn't at his desk. He was sat on one of the uncomfortable looking couches his office held, drinking a cup of tea. It paused, midway to his mouth, when I walked in. Sejin was right behind me.

"Forgive the intrusion, father," Sejin quickly apologized.

He grabbed my wrist and tried to tug me out of there, but I jerked it free. "Grab me again, and I will punch you," I told him calmly.

"What is the meaning of this family visit?" Woojin asked, walking over to us. "Holly, so nice to see your face."

I wish I could say the feeling was mutual.

No, that was a lie. I didn't even wish for that.

"I'm just here to clarify a few things," I told him, completely ignoring the family related things I wanted no part of.

"Holly has made all the artists at Atlantis share social media posts of H3RO!" Sejin jumped in.

I was ready to say that I hadn't forced *anyone* to share anything, much less everyone, but I bit my tongue. I didn't want to get Youngbin or anyone else in trouble, and I had no idea how Woojin would react to any of this. Seeing as he was Sejin's father, and given how he had treated my mother, I wasn't expecting sunshine and cherry blossoms. "H3RO are also Atlantis Entertainments' artists," I said instead. "I don't see how other Atlantis Entertainment artists sharing their own sunbae's accounts could be an undesirable thing. Hell, I've seen a few from JYP and FNC Entertainment sharing and commenting too—and they're the competition!"

"It will result in groups losing their fan base. When that goes, the level of sales drops, which effects our bottom line."

"Oh, bullshit," I snapped at him. "Onyx are not going to lose their fans. They are the most popular group this company has. What's going to happen is they will share the love so Onyx fans also become H3RO fans. When that happens, the level of sales increase because as well as buying Onyx albums and merch and attending *their* concerts and fan meets, they also buy H3RO albums and merch and attend H3RO concerts and fan meets, which effects our bottom line; in a positive way!"

"That is ridiculous," Sejin snapped.

I rolled my eyes. "So's your face," I retorted, in

English. I wasn't sure just how good Sejin's English was, but judging from his expression, he had a vague understanding of my terrible comeback. It wasn't that I didn't know how to translate that, just that my frustration left me floundering. I turned to Woojin and narrowed my eyes. "I have no idea why you insisted I come here and work in this company, but if you really want me to give this a decent effort, you really need to get that asshole on a leash and let me do my job."

"I realize you have been brought up in a country where language like that is acceptable, but here, in this country, in this family, you will speak to your elders with the respect they deserve," Woojin warned me.

I folded my arms, swaying my head like an unimpressed Valley girl. "Don't you dare start commenting on my upbringing when you've had nothing to do with me or my mother for the entirety of my life. And as for respect, I don't give a damn how old a person is: if they're a decent human being, that person will be treated with respect regardless of whether they are older or younger. Until Sejin can act like a decent human being, I will treat him like the asshole he is."

"Your brother—"

"He is not my brother," I cut Woojin off angrily.

"Your *brother* has been learning from me personally for the last ten years," Woojin continued. "We are one of the top five entertainment companies in this country and have been for the last half decade. Despite your opinions, you cannot argue with that fact."

"Just because something has been surviving successfully doesn't mean there isn't room for improvement. And I'm now even questioning that," I added, angry at the fact I was now having to agree verbally to the fact my *father* and *brother* had been doing a pretty good job at running a company I didn't like. "My issues lie in the fact that Sejin wants me to perform a miracle and get a group a number one single when I'm not even getting the support to do it."

"Has it occurred to you that the reason I am making this challenging for you is to see exactly what you are capable of?" Sejin asked, slyly.

I turned to face him, my eyes narrowing. At that moment, I really wished it was possible to kill someone with a stare, instead of just calling it a death glare. "You're not just challenging me, Sejin!" I cried. "You are putting the future of six talented individuals on the line based solely on *my* success or failure."

"What were the terms?" Woojin cut me off again, this time showing a modicum of interest in what was being said.

"I have to get H3RO a number one single," I said.

"Two number ones," Sejin corrected me. "And you set that term by yourself."

Gritting my teeth, I turned to Woojin. "I am trying to do this with zero support, financially, or even just advice-wise, from this company. Yet, when I find a way to raise funds to give this stupid project a half decent shot at actually succeeding; I am constantly getting yelled at and berated by Sejin. If there really is no chance of help coming from Atlantis Entertainment, I, nor H3RO cannot be penalized for thinking outside the box." I turned to Sejin fixing him another glare. "If you think doing a KpopKonneKt campaign is an embarrassment to the company, you might want to let the company give some support, because that's the actual embarrassment. And if you want to talk about *real* embarrassment, having to travel to the other side of the country because there's no recording studio available is ridiculous."

"Is this true?" Woojin asked his son, as though he thought I could be making it up.

"The schedules have been set," Sejin responded although he did look slightly uncomfortable.

"For groups and idols who are currently promoting their current comebacks!" I cried, stamping my foot. It was a childish action, but I was frustrated, and I couldn't stop myself. This family was the most infuriating thing in my life.

"I assume this KpopKonneKt campaign has provided enough money for the recording and music video?" Woojin asked.

I nodded. "No thanks to Sejin," I muttered. "We should have enough to cover that, but I don't know about the music shows. If we didn't have to leave the city and pay what I'm sure is a jacked-up price," I shot Sejin another glare, "I think we would also have enough money for some music shows too, which would help things."

"Schedules cannot be changed at this late notice," Woojin told me, firmly. Before I could say what I was going to (and it was going to be a stream of expletives), he added, "But I will see to it the budget is looked at for promotions. If you can provide the finished article, I will ensure that H3RO have the budget to appear on the music shows. You just have to book them." Woojin walked back behind his desk. "Now, if you would excuse me, I have work to do. Next time, please do not barge into my office like you did today."

"Thank you, father," Sejin said, bowing low at the

man. Like hell I was doing that. Seeing it wasn't going to happen, Sejin reached over and clamped a hand around my wrist, dragging me out of the room. The second we passed through the doorway and into the waiting area where there was a slim chance someone would see us, he released me. "Don't you dare ever try anything like that with me again," Sejin leaned in close so no one could hear him and hissed in my ear. "Or I will see to it that not only will H3RO be disbanded, but they will never work in this industry again."

Leaving me feeling like I had been punched in the gut, Sejin walked away. I stood, staring after him, shaking. Part of it was from anger. I was still livid, and I didn't think that feeling would go away any time soon, but I was also … scared … terrified!

"Are you OK?" a voice asked.

I let out an undignified squeal and spun around. It was Youngbin. He held his hands up, taking a step back. I realized he wasn't alone. Next to him was Jun, staring at me with an expression I couldn't read. I quickly nodded, clearing my throat as I tried to regain my composure. "I'm fine," I said, hoping that he would believe me.

The look Youngbin gave me said he didn't. "Just so you know, the doors in this company aren't all that thick."

I could feel the blood rushing from my head, and I staggered over to the sofa which took up a good portion of the waiting area. Opposite, Woojin's secretary busied himself with something on his computer, intentionally keeping his attention anywhere but on me. Youngbin perched down beside me, while Jun stood just behind him, watching.

"Not here," Youngbin said, pulling me back up to my feet. "Look, gossip doesn't tend to leave this building, but it does spread around it like wildfire," Youngbin told me as he led me back to my office.

I spent the entire short walk praying that I wouldn't pass out or throw up—it was getting close to one or both of those things happening. Safely in my office, I sank onto the floor in front of my sofa, leaning back against it. I didn't trust myself not to pass out still and the less distance between my head and the floor, the better. "How much did you hear?" I asked.

"Enough to know that H3RO are damn lucky to have you as their manager, fighting in their corner," Youngbin replied.

I sank my head into my hands. "I would say they were the exact opposite of lucky, right now."

"Youngbin is right," Jun said, finally speaking up. "Of everyone who could be our manager, I'm glad it's you."

I sucked in a breath, still fighting the nausea despite his words. I looked up at them through my fingers. "Is that supposed to fill me with confidence?"

"I know this is going to be hard to hear, but your father isn't a bad guy."

Hard to hear was an understatement. "You know he's my father?" I whispered. *Oh god* … I couldn't even bring myself to look at Jun. "You can't tell anyone. I can't have the rest of H3RO finding that out," I begged him as I turned to face them. "Please, don't tell the others."

Jun slowly licked his lower lip. "You don't think it's something they should know?"

I shook my head. "I hate hiding this from you," I

told him. "But I've only just managed to convince Tae and Kyun that I'm not here to disband you. If they find out, they will think I'm some mole sent in by my … by Sejin, to find as much dirt on them as possible, or worse! Please, Jun. Let me get you the number one you deserve and then I will tell them."

제12 장

H3RO

Can You Feel It?

"Well," said Youngbin, rubbing at the back of his neck. "This is clearly a conversation I no longer need to be a part of. I'm going to go and let you two talk." He took a couple of steps to the door, then stopped, turning back. He leaned over, resting his forearms on the back of the couch to look at me. "Recording studios!"

I looked up at him, pulling my attention away from H3RO's maknae. "Recording studios?"

"I have one scheduled for the rest of the week, but I'm only working on a mixtape. H3RO can use it, and I'm not GiriBoy, but I've been producing some of Onyx's stuff. I'd be happy to help out with that."

"I could hug you right now," I told him.

Youngbin glanced behind me, then back to me. "Next time. You two need to talk first. I'll text you later," he added before leaving Jun and I alone in my office.

I watched the door close behind him, before turning back to Jun. He had moved so he was perched on the coffee table, his elbows resting on his knees as he stared at me. I let out a deep sigh. "I'll tell them later," I told him. I couldn't ask him to keep it from his group. That was unreasonable of me.

He chewed at his lower lip as he stared at me, mulling it over. Then he shook his head. "Maybe you should hold off on that for a while."

"No," I said, frowning. "Asking you to keep that secret is unfair," I told him. "I'm sorry: I shouldn't have asked that of you."

"But it makes sense," he said, slowly. "Kyun is … he doesn't need to know this just yet. I don't think he will handle that news very well."

I closed my eyes and wrapped my arms around myself. If I was being honest, there was relief washing over me, despite the guilt I felt at the idea of Jun *and* Nate both knowing this secret. For the umpteenth time, I found myself wondering what I was doing here. I was in completely over my head and there were people's futures hanging in the balance.

All I wanted to do was cry. It was starting to get too much for me, and the amount of stress that came with the responsibility was churning away at me.

The sofa dipped behind me, and before I could work out what was happening, Jun had reached down, pulled me onto his lap and wrapped his arms around me. "What are you doing?" I hissed, trying to wriggle free.

Jun's grip tightened and he pulled my side against his chest. "You look like you're struggling to keep it all in, so I'm here to help," he murmured into my ear. "Just relax."

"Jun, I can't," I objected, still trying to free

myself.

"Ten minutes," he said. "I'm not asking for the world."

I stopped squirming, but still tensed, turned my head. Our faces were inches from each other. "I can't, Jun," I said my voice barely louder than a whisper. "I'm not sure I can be satisfied with only ten minutes."

Jun's eyes darkened, but it wasn't anger I saw there.

That look was going to turn me to mush.

That look was going to make me do something I shouldn't.

That look was going to win. I couldn't look away.

"Who said you only had to have ten minutes?" he said, softly.

He leaned forward, making the small gap between us disappear. Slowly, gently, his lips started moving against mine. He tasted of strawberry chap stick. Any thought of fighting it disappeared from my brain with that realization and I closed my eyes, letting my own body take over.

Our lips were moving at a steady pace. Like he was casting a spell over me, I could feel all the stress start to leave me. Forget about ten minutes. I was willing to spend eternity with the slow, almost teasing, kisses, and his arms holding me like he never wanted to let me go. Holy hell, he tasted good and I couldn't get enough of him.

I tilted my head, trying to deepen the kiss, but the angle was awkward. As though he sensed the discomfort, he wrapped his hands around my waist and lifted me. Briefly, we parted, and I stared down at him as he held me above him. Then, I raised my leg, just enough so that when he lowered me, I was straddling him.

Jun reached up, gently tucking some of my hair behind my ear. "You're beautiful," I told him.

"I think that's supposed to be my line," he said, arching an eyebrow. "I'm supposed to be manly and handsome."

"You're that too," I agreed.

I let out a long breath, but he shook his head at me. "Whatever you're thinking: don't."

I stared down at him, wondering how he could possibly know what I was thinking. Yet, I wanted to do as he suggested. My brain was going into the 'you're his manager' territory.

He gently shook his head again, then reached a hand up to cup the back of my neck. He pulled me back to him. I ignored my instinct to listen to my brain and returned his kiss. The hell with it.

His hand left my face, settling on my thigh. The other one quickly mirrored it. The skirt to my dress had a slight flair to it, which had risen up when I had maneuvered myself into this position. While Jun's fingers were settled safely on the fabric, his palm, hot and smooth, were resting on my bare skin. My hands moved from his shoulders to caress the hard lines of his chest.

Slowly, Jun's hands slipped under the skirt and began sliding higher up my legs. As they reached around my butt, my own hands shot down to grab his. I pulled away to find him staring at me in a way which had me both regretting pulling away and being exceptionally grateful.

"Is this the part where you tell me you're my

manager and then I tell you I don't care?" he asked me, his voice gruff.

"This is the part where I tell you that we are in my office and the door is unlocked," I said with a shake of my head.

"I can fix that!" Jun exclaimed, his hands, still under my skirt, gliding up to my waist, ready to lift me again.

I shook my head and placed my hands back on his shoulders. "Not today, Jun."

He gave me a smirk. "That implies there will be another time."

I closed my eyes, then, surprised at the effort it was taking, stepped off the sofa, and out of his lap. "We should get back," I told him, without responding to his suggestion.

The truth was, I wasn't really bothered that I was his manager. My greater concern was Nate. I had spent a week looking forward to his goodnight kisses. I had accepted there was an attraction there. I had conceded to the fact I was prepared to let more of that happen.

And now, here I was, making out with Jun.

I hadn't made a commitment to either of them, but I felt like I was cheating on one with the other. I needed to step back from this and work out what I was doing, because I was not that kind of girl.

… That would have maybe been convincing if I hadn't just made out with Jun.

Holy hell, what was I doing?

Maybe being their manager was what I really did need—and to enforce it. If not, I was sure someone was going to get hurt.

"We should get back and let the others know

about the recording studio," Jun said, as though he knew what I was thinking.

I had to keep myself from narrowing my eyes at him. I had a sneaky suspicion that Jun was a lot more perceptive than I thought and that had the potential to be dangerous.

I straightened my skirt as Jun rose, standing in front of me. I looked up and found him staring down at me, that dark, heated look back in his eyes. Quickly, I cleared my throat and stepped back. "We should pick up some food on the way back."

"I like you," Jun declared, suddenly.

I stood blinking at him. "I like you too," I responded.

"No, I *like* you," he said again. He took a step towards me, brushing my hair back from my face.

"I ..." I was caught in his gaze. "I like you too," I said again.

"You think too much about things," he murmured. "Maybe you should just let things happen. It might surprise you." He leaned forward and kissed me, then stepped back. "You might like it," he added. He stepped back again, giving me space. "Maybe you should just find what you want? Put yourself out there."

"Didn't I say that?" I asked, arching an eyebrow at him.

"When wise words are spoken, they should be shared," Jun declared.

I didn't know about wise words, and even if they were, they were said with a different context. Finding what I wanted was probably going to result in someone getting hurt. I sucked in a breath and straightened my back. I was going to do what I did best and ignore the situation. For now, at least. Maybe, being back in Seoul, back in the dorm, things would be different with Nate anyway. It wasn't like I was stealing his bed anymore.

"Let's go," I said to Jun.

It was a pleasant evening, and the streets were still reasonably busy. Outside, there were still a few fans lurking, but the two that had been there earlier for H3RO had gone. That was a shame. I would have liked for Jun to have seen that. Then again, it was probably safer for Jun that they hadn't seen him.

There would come a point soon when they would have to use the other exit. I was sure of that. As we walked away from the Atlantis Entertainment building, Jun's hand slipped into mine. I stared down at it but didn't do anything to remove it. Instead, I kept my attention on the street ahead of me, though I could see Jun smirking from the corner of my eye.

What in the holy hell was I doing?

H3RO

"Where?" Dante asked in surprise.

"One of Atlantis' recording studios," I said, repeating myself.

"But I thought they were booked out?" Tae asked, suspicion lining his eyes.

I nodded. "Technically, they are, but Youngbin said he was only using it to work on his mixtape. He's happy for you guys to use it this week. He's also offered to help you out with producing the album."

Tae sat there, staring at me, still as a statue. Internally, I sighed. Outwardly, I took another bite of my sub. Jun and I had called in at a Subway on our way back and picked up a sandwich for everyone. While we had sat eating at the table, I had told them that they were going into the studio in the morning. Tae was the only one that didn't seem happy. I had a suspicion that it was because his supposed hoobae was the one who was going to be doing the producing.

Tae rolled up the remainder of his sandwich and got up, leaving the room. Kyun started to get up to follow, but I shook my head. "Leave this one with me," I told him, firmly.

I hurried after Tae, knocking on his bedroom door. I didn't wait for an answer before walking in. I quickly shut the door behind me, then turned to face Tae. He was shirtless. My mouth fell open. I'd seen it before when he'd been at the pool, but the hard lines were an impressive (and yes, drool-worthy) sight.

"Oh!" he exclaimed, finally looking at me.

"Sorry," I murmured, making myself look him in the eyes.

"I thought you were Kyun-*ah*," he said with a shrug. He reached over for his T-shirt, pulling it back on.

The spell broken, I shook my daydreams from my head. "It's because you're his sunbae, right?" I asked him. I wasn't going to beat around the bush. "Youngbin. You're older than him, and you debuted before him, right?"

Slowly, Tae nodded. "It doesn't feel right."

"He's doing it *because* you're his sunbae," I pointed out. "He wants H3RO to succeed. He wants you, his friend—his *hyung*—to succeed." I gave him what I hoped was a reassuring smile. "I know it might feel strange, but he wants to work with you. Or if you have no desire to produce yourself, one of the others. And if none of you want to, that's fine, he can do it. But he knows you guys, and he's had some success himself. I know he's not a full-time producer, but he has an idea of what he's doing—he got Onyx a number one with the last single."

Tae rubbed at the bridge of his nose. "Holly," he sighed. "This isn't America."

"I know it's not," I said. "I know this makes you uncomfortable, but at this point, I can't find you any alternative, so for lack of a more fitting Korean saying, *suck it up*. Right now, the important thing is H3RO, and if that means working with Youngbin to give you your best shot, I'm prepared to do that, and you've got to do it too. Otherwise you do it yourself."

"Very well," Tae sighed. He still didn't look comfortable at that decision, but that was for him to work through.

제 13 장

H3RO

What Am I To You?

I sat in the minibus, drumming my hands on the steering wheel. For the last three days H3RO had been in the recording studio. Last night, Minhyuk had excitedly declared that they probably only needed one more day to finish recording before Youngbin and Tae disappeared to work on bringing the songs together.

I was excited for them, but I had also told them expressly that tonight, they were to leave that studio no later than six. It was twenty after already, and there was nobody in this minibus with me.

Tonight, was the night Inhye's brother-in-law was going to give them all their comeback makeover. This weekend, Kate was coming back, and we were going to take their concept photos.

Everything was moving to schedule.

Only, there wasn't a concept.

And that wasn't the only problem: I still had no music video director.

Honestly, I was sure I was about to have a

nervous breakdown. I was struggling to get any real sleep, and when Nate kept providing me with food and drinks at regular intervals (I kept losing track of time), I had very little appetite and would only pick at what was given to me, just to keep Nate happy.

Thankfully, I had told the guys that they needed to be finished at six, when in reality, they needed to be out by seven—just in case—but I was getting angsty. Jae, Inhye's brother-in-law was doing us a huge favor, staying open late and doing this. I didn't want to push my luck.

I got out of the minibus, ready to head in and to the studio, but thankfully Minhyuk and Jun burst out of the door, chatting excitedly. Nate and Dante were right behind them. Minhyuk stopped when he saw me. "Oh, we're late!"

"It's OK," I said, hurriedly. "Just get in the minibus and we can go." I looked behind the four with a frown. "Where are Tae and Kyun?" I asked.

Nate looked over his shoulder and then shrugged. "Tae said he wanted to record Kyun's part one last time. They should be out soon."

I drummed my fingers against the side of the minibus, and then shook my head. "We need to go," I muttered. "You guys get in the minibus. I'll go get them. They can finish recording tomorrow."

I stepped past the group with a sigh and entered the building. Seconds later, there were footsteps hurrying after me. "Holly!" Nate called.

"You should wait in the bus," I said, not stopping as I responded to him.

Nate let out a frustrated grunt, then grabbed my wrist, stopping me and pulling me back. "You look like you're going to implode. Or explode," he shrugged. "Is everything OK?"

"It would be OK if you guys could stick to a schedule. Clearly, I need to keep a closer eye on you, and manage you better," I said with a frown.

"I'm worried about you," he admitted. "I don't think you're getting enough sleep or eating well."

I shrugged. "Don't you worry about me. When this comeback hits, you won't be sleeping for days, never mind eating at correct times. If you guys can do it, so can I."

"I know our schedules will get crazy, and I'm looking forward to that," Nate admitted. He still had hold of my wrist. "But you're missing the fact that when we are busy, we try to catch as much sleep as we can, where we can. We also make sure to eat properly when we do it. You're doing neither."

"I've got to get your comeback in order," I shrugged again. "I can sleep when you're performing."

"You'd miss our performances?" Nate asked, screwing up his nose in displeasure. "That's not right. We need you there. So, we need you looking after yourself now, so you can be."

The hand around my wrist slipped down and then he was holding my hand. As though he was using it to anchor me in place, Nate bowed forward and kissed me. I pulled back, though didn't get too far with him still holding on to me. "Nate, what are you doing?"

He winced. "I thought I was kissing you, but if you have to ask, I'm clearly doing a bad job of it."

"Not at all," I quickly told him. "You're a good kisser," I assured him. "I just ... we shouldn't be doing this here, and we need to get to the salon. Plus, I'm not stealing your bed anymore."

Nate blinked at me a few times, then reached for my other hand. "Holly, I never needed payment for you taking my bed. I was just using that as an excuse to kiss you. Now, I don't need any excuses. I'm just going to kiss you."

"Nate," I sighed. "Much as I would love to stand here kissing you all evening, we have to get to the salon and—" I let out a squeal as I was suddenly pulled through a closed door. The next thing I knew, I was pressed up against it. "What are you doing?" I asked, even though my heart was racing.

"I just told you," he whispered, before leaning down to steal a kiss. When he pulled away, he gave me a cheeky grin. "I'm going to be doing that a lot more."

"OK," I said, before my hands flew to my mouth. That earned me another smile and when I dropped my hands away from my lips, another kiss. A kiss I didn't protest to, but one I should have done.

"I'll wait in the minibus," Nate said, leaving me alone.

I ran my fingers over my lower lip. I needed to decide what to do about Nate and Jun, but now was not that time. Right now, I needed to find Tae and Kyun and get H3RO to Itaewon where Jae's salon was.

I left the room, only to find Tae and Kyun walking down the corridor towards me. "You're late," I pointed out.

"But we've finished recording," Kyun responded. I had to force myself to not stare at him: it was slight, but there was a smile there.

"Which we can celebrate later, but right now, we're already behind schedule.

Like that, the smile disappeared, and Kyun looked instantly uncomfortable.

"That's my fault," Tae spoke up straight away.

"I'm not looking to place blame," I shrugged. "I just need you to pick up the pace. Let's go."

I hurried for the door. Outside, I would have been able to narrow down our minibus even if I didn't have a clue which one it was. It was the only vehicle with Big Bang blasting from it. Inside, the four occupants were dancing and singing in their seats. This was the most animated I'd seen them for some time.

"Did you get finished, hyung?" Jun called from the backseat.

"All done," Tae agreed.

A boisterous cheer momentarily drowned out G-Dragon. I couldn't help but smile to myself as we left the Atlantis underground parking lot. We were getting closer to finishing this album and it was feeling more and more real for all of us.

I let Dante, who was with me in the front, keep control of the iPod we had plugged in, as we drove to Itaewon. He kept the beat up-tempo and I was kept entertained by everyone singing along to whatever was being played. They really did have incredible voices.

I pulled up as close to the salon as I could get. Still in high spirits, the guys tumbled out of the minibus and headed towards the salon. I stopped when I realized the shutters were down.

The cheerful atmosphere evaporated. "Are we too late?" Kyun asked beside me. He had gone pale.

"This isn't your fault," Tae assured him, though he shot me a questioning look.

I glanced at my watch. It was only a few minutes

later than the time I had agreed with Jae. "I'm sure there's an explanation," I said, stepping forward to hammer at the shutters.

Minutes later they shot up. A man emerged from within with a wide smile on his face. "Holly? And H3RO? Please do come in." He stepped back to allow us to enter. Inside was lit up and six stations were set up. Lurking in the background was a girl not much younger than me.

Behind me, the shutters clattered down, making me jump backwards into Nate. His hand shot forward onto the small of my back. "Easy," he murmured in my ear.

"My apologies," Jae said. "I have a glass fronted shop and I wanted to give H3RO privacy tonight. No need for spoilers."

"Thank you," I said, grateful he had thought of that.

"Gentlemen, make yourself comfortable while I discuss things with your manager. There are drinks and snacks in the kitchen." Jae gave me a bright smile and then led me into a small room in the back. It was a bit cluttered, but there was a small desk there. "Inhye filled me in with what has been happening with H3RO at Atlantis and I want to start by assuring you that you will have my absolute discretion. She gave me a Non-Disclosure Agreement which I have signed."

He picked up a sheet of paper from his desk and handed it over. I scanned over the NDA. It looked like an official Atlantis document. Given that it had come from Inhye, I was sure it was above board. "Thank you."

"She also mentioned that you have been having

trouble booking people to work for you. Have you found someone to produce your music video?"

My eyes went wide at that. Just how much did Atlantis know? Then again, Inhye was Sejin's secretary, so she probably knew a hell of a lot that went on at Atlantis. "No."

"Forgive me if I've spoken out of turn," he said, bowing his head. "Inhye and my wife, her sister, are very close. As she is still single, she spends a lot of time at our place, and she has always spoken highly of H3RO. Did you know she went to school with Tae?"

I nodded. "She mentioned that."

"Then let me add my reassurances that we want H3RO to succeed too. Which is why I asked about the music video. One of my clients is a very talented individual. She's done a lot of videos and is currently studying the subject at the Seoul Leadership University. She is unknown, but she is willing and eager to help you out."

I sat down in the chair, heavily, and rubbed at my neck. "Has she ever done a music video before?" I asked him, doubtful.

"No," he admitted. "But she is very talented."

I had nothing against emerging talent, and unknown names. I was here with Jae, after all, who had only recently started up this salon. But was the risk of letting an unknown—a student—make the music video worth it for not just myself and H3RO, but for her too?

OK, it was possible that H3RO could walk out of here with a tragic haircut, but it would grow back. I was also prepared to pull scissors out of Jae's hands if I needed to. Even then, with a discussion first, as to what was going to happen to the hair, it was unlikely that anything too bad could happen.

The music video was different. This could make or break the song.

But, despite H3RO's seniority in the K-Pop world, there was no one out there willing to work with them. That wasn't their fault. That was Sejin's.

"Would you like to meet her first, before committing?" he suggested. "Hear her idea."

"Yes," I nodded. "I would very much like that."

Jae pushed the door open. "Ahn Soomi?"

Seconds later, we were joined by a girl. She was about my height, with ridiculously long dark hair. It fell nearly to her butt with a glossy sheen. She had wide eyes with a single eyelid, and a heart shaped mouth. She was easily pretty enough to be an idol herself. "Hello," she bowed.

"Jae said you wanted to produce H3RO's music video."

Soomi blinked a few times, then nodded her head. "I do," she said, so quietly, I struggled to hear her.

"The floor is all yours."

"I have an idea," she said, still quiet. I leaned forward with a frown. "Of course, it depends on the song, but I think it could work for something up-tempo, or a ballad," she explained. "I want to tell a story. I want it to go over three videos—the start, the middle, and the end—like a story's arch does."

"You want to make three videos?" I asked, my eyebrow shooting up. "Do you not think that's a little bold?"

"If I'm going to ask for one, I might as well ask for three," she shrugged. She still spoke quietly, but there was a confidence there. "But if you decide to go in a different direction with their next single, then I will understand. If you want to, I'll even let you continue with my idea with another director."

There was something about her that I liked. "What are your terms?"

"I want my name on the music video," she declared, loudly, then seeming surprised at her own voice, continued at a quieter volume. "I would also like permission to use it as my project submission. Price wise, I would like to cover my expenses, but I will keep them as low as possible."

"What about crew and equipment?"

"You will need to cover the cost for some of the equipment. Some I have. I will use my own crew."

"What's the story idea?"

I looked up and found Tae in the doorway. I arched an eyebrow but said nothing. He was H3RO's leader, after all. Considering he had written the song and was going to be a part of producing it, he was completely entitled to have a say on the video. I was also encouraged at the fact he wasn't shooting her down, especially as he had probably heard most of the conversation.

He folded his arms and listened intently as Soomi explained her concept. By the end of her description, I was sold. Her idea would work regardless of the song, but, having heard the rough demo, it felt like she had heard it to. She also seemed to come alive as she described it. She was naturally quiet, but she had the ability to hold a crowd's attention when she talked, especially because her passion was obvious.

I looked over at Tae and smiled when he nodded. "Welcome aboard," I told her.

She let out a giddy squeal, jiggling on the spot. "Thank you. You will not regret this."

I didn't think I would.

Once I had gotten her details from her, she raced out of the room, stating she had to get prepared so we could start work the following week.

Jae clapped his hands in pleasure. "I had spoken to Soomi previously. We had come up with some concepts for H3RO's hair. As there is some coloring involved, I will get started. It will be a late night."

"We don't have to go anywhere, so long as it's not an inconvenience to you," I assured him.

He shook his head, smiling, and then hurried from the room. I sat back in the chair and closed my eyes. It was strange, but in the twenty minutes that conversation had taken, it felt like someone had lifted a crushing weight from me, and until then, I hadn't realized just how heavy it was. Then I sighed. "I probably should have seen what she had done previously," I muttered, to myself.

"I think you made the right decision," Tae said, making me jump as I opened my eyes. I hadn't realized he had stayed in the room.

"I just want the song, and you guys, to have the best video possible. But I loved her idea, and I loved her passion, and most of all, I loved that she was thinking of the next two videos also," I explained. Tae took half a step towards me, then stopped, frowning. "Are you OK?" I asked him, as I got to my feet.

He made to move again, then hesitated. Then he sucked in a deep breath. I tilted my head, trying to work out what he was doing.

Then he leaned down and kissed me.

It was light, and slightly longer than a peck on the lips, but it was kiss.

Just like that, he pulled away. "Thank you," he murmured, before disappearing from the room.

I sank back down onto the chair, my fingers tracing my lips. Tae? Tae kissed me. Tae kissed me? Why was Tae kissing me?

No, I couldn't cope with this. Not him as well.

I laughed out loud at that. *As well.* What alternative universe had I walked into where three insanely gorgeous guys were attracted to me?

Nope, I was not dealing with this one now. Once again, I decided I would ignore it. I had six makeovers to supervise anyway.

제14 장

H3RO

Dress Up

I had expected us to leave the salon with only half of the guys having had a haircut, given how late it was when we started. Instead, Jae stayed open until the early hours of the morning. Between him and Yoo Eunjung, the girl who had been hiding in the shadows when we had arrived, the pair stayed busy. Eunjung, I discovered, was a makeup artist, but she often worked with Jae. Between the two of them, when they had finished, I was in awe.

Awe was the wrong word.

Lust.

I was in lust.

Holy hell, I was in lust.

Over the next few days I had just about managed to bottle that and lock it away in the back of my mind, when the photoshoot happened.

On the weekend, Jae had joined us at a location by the river that Soomi had found us. I'd gotten a trailer and he'd set up base there, ready to touch up and restyle hair as and when it was needed. He'd also brought along

Yoo Eunjung, and they had spent the last few hours doing their makeup with only a little guidance from myself, Soomi and Kate.

Today was the day for the photos, hence Kate being present. Soomi had volunteered to come down so she could help Kate set the tone so there would be a connection to the video. She was also going to take some behind the scenes footage for us to use at another point in time. While the guys were getting their makeup done, I had spent the time translating between the two of them.

We'd started at 2 a.m. because we wanted to get some shots with the sunrise, and as such none of us had gone to bed. I'd poked my head into the trailer at several points, relieved to find H3RO were taking it in turns to nap. Outside, Kate, Soomi and I were running off energy drinks and excitement: as I'd been translating, the three of us were feeding off each other's enthusiasm.

Soomi also had a student friend who was a fashion designer. Or at least, he was trying to be a designer. He was at the Seoul Leadership University with Soomi and desperate to break out with his concepts. Apparently, as soon as Soomi had let him know I was happy for him to join the team, he had spent all week locked in a classroom, making adjustments to some designs he already had, following Soomi's concepts.

I was nervous, but equally, looking forward to seeing them. I couldn't wait to see how all this was going to come together.

There was some noise at the trailer, and the three of us turned.

"Fuck me," Kate muttered under her breath, her camera already in front of her eyes as she took shots of the guys leaving the trailer one by one.

I couldn't find any words. The lust I thought I had locked away had broken free and taken over all ability for me to form anything close to a coherent sentence. Honestly, I was impressed I managed to keep my mouth from falling open and drooling everywhere.

I'd seen them all with bed hair, scruffy clothes, unshaved, fresh from a work out, and having had no sleep at all. H3RO were handsome to start with. But *Holy hell!* With makeup and freshly styled hair, along with their outfits, I will admit I was ready to be completely selfish and drag them all back to the dorm.

Tae had kept his hair dark. It was straightened and parted on his left to show a sliver of forehead. He was sporting a pierced eyebrow (he'd gotten that done last night), and a single, long earring. His top was a faded red—long, with extra-long sleeves—that didn't hide any of his muscles in the slightest. Along with the ripped combat trousers and biker boots, Jae, Eunjung, and the designer had hit the mark with 'trouble'.

Dante stepped out next. "Oh, they have got to be airbrushed on," Kate muttered beside me.

I knew exactly what she was talking about. Dante had slightly wilder looking hair. It fell over his forehead like he had just woken up, but it was one of those hairstyles which had probably been crafted for each lock of hair to fall into place. He was going to hate that before every performance. It was also streaked with a deep red which matched the deep red coat he was wearing. That was it up top. There was no shirt or vest, just his bare chest. And that was what Kate was talking about. "Nope," I informed her. "That is one hundred percent real."

Kate brought her head back from the camera to give me side eye. "Dude, you and I are going to have words later, because not sharing that piece of information is not cool. And also, how on earth do you know he looks like that?"

I waved her comment away. Telling her the whole truth behind that story was embarrassing. Nate was out next. I wanted to yell at him to go back in to give me a little more time to prepare for this. His hair had gone a light brown which made his skin golden. Jae had kept most of the length but had styled it so it was swept up and to the side, showing off the whole of his forehead. Back in the salon I'd seen the bleach and toner being applied, so the color wasn't a surprise, but how it was styled made him look incredible.

Nate had the second most defined torso, though his arms were more muscular than Dante's. He (or I), had been rewarded with him wearing a deep red vest top. It was a shade darker than Dante's hair, and it showed his arms and shoulders off. I had an urge to bite them. "I wonder if he'll let me?"

"Huh?" Kate asked.

My eyes widened. "Nothing!" I squawked, earning myself a strange look. I'd said that aloud?

Minhyuk was right behind Nate, his hands on his shoulders as they stepped down the few stairs from the trailer. He was wearing skinny trousers, the same shade as Dante's. He was the skinniest member of H3RO, and the trousers made his legs look really thin, especially when he stood beside Nate, who also had very defined thighs. Minhyuk's hair was now brown. He'd also kept a lot of the length. Straightened, it gleamed in the bright lights that had been set up. They'd also given him hazel contacts to wear. There was something slightly feminine about his features, and he looked beautiful.

There were a few seconds before Kyun left the trailer and I had to do a double take. His hair was the shortest. It was also silver. Not gray, but a silver that shone. Behind a pair of glasses, he'd been given contacts that made his eyes look like pools of molten metal. Kyun was the only one in trousers that weren't ripped, and he was in an oversized black woolen jumper with thin red stripes which ran down one of the sleeves.

And then Jun appeared. His eyeliner made him look a few years older, in a good way. No, scratch that— in a dangerous way. His hair completely covered his forehead, sitting just below his eyebrows. It was black, but as he moved his head, the dark blue underneath showed. He was the only member in shorts. They ended around his knees. They looked slightly longer on one side due to the red mesh that hung over them. He was also wearing a ripped T-shirt, but he had several pieces of red and black material that wrapped around his right arm.

"It's a good job you can't get pregnant by looking," I heard Kate mutter. I laughed, but I knew exactly what she meant.

"What are you laughing at?" Dante asked, walking over and draping his arm around my shoulder.

"Inside joke. Ask Holly," Kate shrugged, before scurrying off.

I let out a growl and glanced up at Dante. I found him looking at me, expectantly. "We were just agreeing on how good you guys look," I told him.

Dante looked down at himself and nodded. "I know." He gave me a sly grin. "But you already knew how good I look."

I pulled my head back to be able to look him in the eye. "There isn't an inch of you that doesn't look good," I informed him, before calmly walking over to Jae. Well, it looked calm. Inside, my heart was pounding. Was I really flirting with Dante too? I was going to hell.

"They look good," Jae told me as I approached.

"Thanks to you and Eunjung," I agreed. "Thank you," I said to them both.

"I'll stick around in case they need touching up during the shoot," Jae added.

Eunjung looked up at the dark skies. "It's going to rain. They will need their makeup redoing, I'm sure. I will also stay."

She was right. It did rain.

We managed to get a lot of shots in the sunrise, according to Kate. She was more focused on getting group shots on the riverbank with the sun rising behind them. I wasn't a photographer, but standing behind her, seeing things from her angle, I was sure they were going to come out great. She had several cameras she flicked between, including a polaroid camera. "Add them to the KpopKonneKt campaign."

We'd moved to a paved area about half a mile from the trailer and had started on the individual shots when the heavens opened. I'd been ready to call it off, panicking like a mother hen at the idea of everyone being out in the rain, especially with the chilly wind that was coming down the river. I'd balked at the idea of them getting a cold, but both Soomi and Kate had yelled "NO!" at me with such force, it was almost physical as

I stepped back.

"Not going to lie," Kate had called. "These guys look hot as hell when wet."

Well, she wasn't wrong. But it was also cold as anything.

I'd had the foresight to bring some umbrellas with me, so while Kate was photographing Nate, I'd given them to the others and sent them back to the trailer to stay dry and warm.

We didn't have much of a crew with us, so it was down to me and Soomi to do as much as we could. Soomi stood with Kate, sheltering her with a giant umbrella. In between shots, I would run over and wrap a blanket around whoever was being photographed, and make sure they were sufficiently protected from the rain. They were already soaked at that point, so it was more to keep them warm and protected from the wind, than dry.

By the time we were on the last member of H3RO, Tae, I was so cold, I could barely feel my fingers or my feet. My trainers were not waterproof, and the jacket I had been wearing, which was supposed to be waterproof, had leaked in water everywhere. It was also thin and offered little protection from the icy wind.

Kate was busy replacing batteries, a flash and a memory card. I was huddled behind Tae, holding the umbrella at an angle above him, when a particularly strong gust of wind blew down the riverside. I let out a shudder, and Tae whirled around. His jumper was woolen and waterlogged beneath the blanket that was also sodden. "How are you holding up?" I asked him through chattering teeth. "She's nearly finished."

"You're shivering," he said with a frown.

"So are you," I returned. "I'm sorry. The weather said the rain would come later this afternoon."

"The weather is not your fault," he said, quietly.

"You're doing exceptionally well to endure this," I told him.

He stared at me, still frowning, then opened up one side of the blanket. He reached out and pulled me to him, jerking his head out of the way of the umbrella as I stumbled into him with a squeal. Then he wrapped the blanket around us both.

I stood there, hardly daring to breath. After the out-of-the-blue kiss the other night, Tae had been avoiding me. I felt like even breathing would scare him off. And then the shivers set in again. "Sorry," I mumbled into his shoulder as the umbrella jerked against him. I kept my eyes trained on the umbrella handle, trying to keep my hands from shaking.

Tae exhaled deeply, then the arms around me started moving up and down, rubbing at my upper arms. "You haven't stopped since we got here."

"Neither have Kate and Soomi."

"Yes, they have," Tae disagreed. "They have taken several breaks and had a hot drink: drinks you've been running back and forth with."

"I'm OK," I muttered.

"You're cold and wet," he corrected me again. "You need to take care of yourself."

"My job is to take care of you." I looked up at him and frowned. "Literally. That's my job. I'm replaceable. You guys are not H3RO if one of you is not there. Your job is to perform, and you can't do that if you're ill."

"You're not replaceable," Tae told me, slowly.

There was something in his look that was holding

me like a magnet. Just like that, all I wanted to do was stand on my toes and kiss him. If I was reading him correctly, the feeling was mutual. I mean, he had kissed me … right?

"We're ready to go over here!" Kate yelled behind me.

Her voice broke the spell and I jumped away from Tae. "I'll take that," I said, quickly unwrapping the blanket from around him. I gave him a bright smile. "Endure it a little longer. You're almost done."

I walked away, clinging to the sodden blanket. "What in the hell are you doing, Holly?" I asked myself. "You have enough problems with Jun and Nate. And the random flirting with Dante. You're going to have to choose one of them at some point. Some point soon. Because otherwise, someone is going to get hurt." I sighed and hung my head. Why did I have to choose?

제15 장

H3RO

Gotta Go to Work

Kate had given me a memory stick with over two thousand images from the photoshoot alone, photos, I was happy to learn, which had had minimal photoshopping done to them. I had spent hours staring at the images, trying to pick out the best ones. Hell, that was hard. They all looked good.

One night, we had sat in front of the television with my iPad hooked up to it and spent *five* hours picking through the photographs. Thankfully, with a couple of bowls of ramyun and some beers, it had ended up being a fun evening. By the time we had called it a night, we had selected ten of each member for photocards, pop-ups and album pictures.

H3RO had unanimously agreed on an album title of 'Hunted', and that there would be two versions of the album cover: Dark and Light. When I'd mentioned this to Soomi and Kate, they had decided another photoshoot was in order because what we had represented the dark side, but light needed looking at again. Thankfully, we would have time after the music video had been filmed to take the second set of photos while the video was being cut and edited.

Now we were making progress, this was fun. Stressful and nonstop, but so much fun. The other benefit was that myself and H3RO were so busy that I barely saw them. OK, that's a lie. That did kind of suck. However, the flip side meant that I could live in my little land of denial and not worry if I was stringing anyone along.

I didn't see much of H3RO over the next few days. They were busy choreographing and learning the dance for the song, because like everything else that was up against them, there had only been one available choreographer who had only been available for half a day. It had taken some begging and an extortionate fee that I was still bitter about, to be able to get that.

It was only because both Nate and Minhyuk, H3RO's dancers, had assured me that they would be able to choreograph the rest of it that I had been able to relax. Tae and Dante had disappeared into the studio to finish producing the album.

Jun was being a social media king. He was constantly doing Instagram and V lives and posting in the fan café, replying to so many comments that even a few of the media blogs had picked up on it.

Kyun, as far as I could tell, was still on his quest for abs, spending his time in the gym when he wasn't with Nate and Minhyuk, learning the dance.

I was carefully preparing the comeback buildup. I had been updating as many group profiles as possible. They were so hideously out of date, and I really wanted them all to change Jun's name. In addition, I was busy trying to confirm appearances on shows. There was one variety show in particular that I wanted to get H3RO on. It was a new show with three hosts that was proving very popular in the ratings. It was one which I felt would give them an opportunity to shine as individuals as well.

I had taken to sitting out on the roof to work. Wrapped in a blanket under the shelter, the fresh air was needed to keep me awake. It was also peaceful up here. At some point I must have fallen asleep because when I woke up, I was feeling hot. I rubbed at my eyes, trying to get my brain to kick into gear. It was still dark, but something had awoken me, and I couldn't work out what.

"Holly?"

I rubbed at my eyes again, staring up at the blurry figure. My first thought was that it was Nate. He would continue to regularly come up to check on me, bringing drinks and food. This figure was too tall, too slim, and the voice too low and gravelly to be Nate. "Tae?" I questioned, forcing myself to sit up. "What's wrong?"

"Nothing," he said, hurriedly. "I couldn't sleep because of the video, so I decided to get up early and shower. I saw your bedroom door ajar and realized you weren't there, so I got worried."

I slumped back into the cushions, reaching for my phone to check the time. My alarm would be going off to get everyone up soon anyway. I sighed and closed my eyes. I felt like crap. I was so tired that all I wanted to do was sleep the week away, but there was too much to do.

We had two days to shoot a video, and three days to finalize everything for the album so it could go to print. Then we had two more days until D-day. In the meantime, spoiler images still needed releasing and SNS needed updating. There was too much to do to be able to sleep. That would have to wait.

Some extra coffee was what I needed right now. And maybe a shower.

Groaning at the effort, I pulled myself to my feet. I was barely upright before a dizzy spell hit me and I toppled backwards. Strong arms wrapped around me before I could hit the ground, and I reached out to cling to Tae's shirt. "Holly!" he exclaimed in concern.

"I got up too fast," I muttered as I waited for the spinning to stop. "I'll be fine in a minute," I said, sucking in some deep breaths.

"Sit back down," I was instructed as Tae started to lower us both back onto the cushions.

"I'm fine," I said, resisting him. "Honestly."

"Maybe we should get you to a hospital," he said, still concerned.

I looked up at him and pulled a face. "I just got up too fast, Tae. I don't need a hospital. I need a shower, some coffee, and some breakfast. In that order." I smiled up at him as I patted his arm. "I call dibs on the shower first."

I slipped out of his arms and gathered up my belongings. It was already raining, so I dashed over to the door, using my body to shield my electronics from the water. Tae was right behind me and we took the elevator down together. It wasn't until we were at the door that Tae spoke. "You need to look after yourself."

"I am doing no more than you are," I told him. "You said you couldn't sleep, but have you tried, or were you really at the studio working on the album?" I asked. When he didn't respond, I gave him a pointed look. "There's just over a week, and then things will calm down a little, for me at least. Don't worry about me. You worry about you."

I reached for the door to type in the passcode, but Tae's hand shot out and grabbed my wrist. "That's the problem," he told me.

"What is?" I asked, confused.

"You," he replied. "I can't help but worry about you."

"Huh?" I said, dumbly.

Tae let out a long breath, then slowly, his hand slid over my wrist and grasped my hand. He used it to pull me around to face him. "I worry about you," he said again.

"You don't need to do that," I said.

"But I want to," he murmured, his voice becoming even lower.

I licked my lips … I wanted him to, too.

I wasn't sure who made the first move, but in the next moment, we were kissing. And then I was pinned up against the wall, clutching at Tae's top as his hands wove through my hair. When I gasped, he pulled away, but before I could protest, he was nipping at my ear, his hands leaving my hair and splaying out over my neck and collar bone.

They moved lower, running over my breasts. A moan escaped me. "I like that sound," he whispered into my ear as his hands continue to move over me, rubbing and squeezing. His mouth moved to mine, and then his leg was pushing its way between mine, giving me the friction, I didn't realize I desperately needed.

And then the god damn alarm on my phone went off. "Ignore it," Tae instructed me, as he bit my ear.

The alarm continued to blare away and with a

willpower I had no idea existed, I shook my head. "Damnit," I grunted in frustration. "Tae, that's for the music video. We can't ignore it."

Tae pulled back, allowing his hands to glide down to my waist. He leaned forward, resting his lips against the crook of my neck as he began leaving a line of soft kisses over my skin until he found my mouth. With one last, lingering kiss, he finally stepped back, his eyes still heavy. "I don't start things and not finish them," he promised me.

"Oh, I hope not," I murmured. I reached for the phone and turned the alarm off. "Go shower. I'll wake the others up," I instructed him, although that was the last thing going through my head.

He nodded, typing in the code, then stepped through the door. I took a deep breath, and before the door closed behind him, followed him into the dorm. Inside, I found Jun leaning against the kitchen counter, watching me.

His expression was guarded, but I had a feeling he knew exactly what had been happening in the corridor. Guilt flooded me. "Oh, you're up?" I said.

Jun nodded, slowly. "Yeah. I have been for a little while."

He *definitely* knew what had happened outside of that door.

"We need to leave soon, so you might want to join the queue for the shower," I said, before getting out of there as quickly as I could. I fled to my bedroom and dropped onto my bed. I was going to hell.

H3RO

Everyone was awake and ready within the hour. I hadn't managed to grab that shower, but Tae had certainly done a better job at waking me up ... and working me up. The drive to the first shoot location was uncomfortable for a whole host of reasons. Not least because I could see Jun in the rearview mirror and his eyes never left me the whole way there.

We had three locations to visit today, and another two tomorrow—though they were just outside of Seoul. The first location was an abandoned building. I recognized it from a few other music videos as we walked in. While Soomi and I organized the lighting with a few techs she had brought with her, the guys were in another room with Jae and Eunjung. We finished around the same time, and then it was time to shoot.

The first part of the filming was to take place outside in the surrounding streets, while the lighting was right. The whole area was industrial but vacant. According to Soomi, it was perfect for the dystopian feel she wanted. Unfortunately, it was raining cats and dogs.

It matched with the shots we had done earlier in the week, but I couldn't help but feel sorry for everyone who was involved. We were all drenched within minutes. The only upside was that compared to last time, away from the river and protected by the buildings, it was considerably warmer. I made sure everyone had a blanket and hot drinks between shots, and I'd also made sure to bring several large heaters for everyone to congregate around.

I stood back to one side, watching. Soomi had described the three-arc video plot to me. This one, although the first we would shoot and release, was actually the second part to the story. H3RO were on the run, hiding from their pursuers. It wouldn't be until the third video that the story would reveal why they were being hunted. Soomi has sketched it all out in a storyboard, then chopped it up for me to see. I loved her idea.

When we had explained it to H3RO, they had gotten excited too. That was until they were filming. By the second location, I could see how tired they were getting. Minhyuk, was especially struggling from all the running, but not once did any of them complain. I was proud of them. I had no idea where their reputation of being unprofessional had come from. They were being anything but.

When the groups split up into pairs, I hurried over to Minhyuk with a soda and a banana. "You're doing well," I told him.

"I'm not a runner," he said, sounding as exhausted as he looked.

"I think most of the running is done with." I crouched down next to him and started massaging his legs.

His eyes went wide. "What are you doing?"

My hands shot away. "I'm sorry. I didn't mean to overstep the line."

"No, it's OK. It just startled me," he said, slowly.

I sat on the floor, crossing my legs, and reached for his again. Gently, I began rubbing his calves. "Make the most of this break though."

"That sounds like an excellent idea," Jun declared, joining us. He sat down beside Minhyuk, then lay his head down in Minhyuk's lap. "I'm going to nap," he added, before closing his eyes. Within minutes, he was snoring.

I arched an eyebrow at Minhyuk. "Really?"

Minhyuk shrugged. "He can sleep anywhere at any time. I'm jealous, actually." He reached down and started playing with Jun's hair, moving the black aside so he could see the inky blue dye underneath. "I like this blue." He frowned. "Does this mean we have the same hair for the next song?"

I shook my head. "Look at BTS or Monsta X, or even GOT7. They have continuing storylines which are far more complex than ours, and they've looked different in all of them. If you want to keep what you have, do. If not, let's change it up."

Minhyuk's fingers teased at Jun's hair, but he was watching Dante. "I think I'd like to try red next."

"Holly!" One of the techs called.

I sighed and got to my feet and hurried over to where the shout had originated from. So much for my own break.

H3RO

By the end of second day, I was dead on my feet. Our final location, while threatening to rain all day, had remained dry, although cool. Most of this day was spent with H3RO performing the routine again and again. Hearing it aloud in the *almost* finished state (Tae, while filming the previous day, had decided something needed changing, and was going to do that tonight so that Soomi could get started on the video tomorrow) and seeing the dance they'd come up with was an exhilarating feeling.

"I need a foot massage," Jun grumbled, swirling

in his seat to put his feet in Minhyuk's lap.

"Ew!" Minhyuk exclaimed, pushing them off him.

"Hyung!" Jun whined drawing out the word.

Dante leaned forward between the seats and clipped Jun around the back of the head. "Behave."

I was trying to get them all into the minibus to take them home and had only succeeded in getting those three in. There were moments like this where I was sure 'manager' was just another way of saying 'babysitter'.

I moved to the side and leaned back against the front passenger door, out of the way. Over the last forty-eight hours alone, I was firing on four hours sleep. I was exhausted. We only had a couple of hours until we were back at the dorm, and then the evening was ours. My plan consisted of food, shower, and an early night.

I sucked in a deep breath as a dizzy spell washed over me. Food was first on that list. I fished a chocolate bar from out of my pocket and started eating it. Then my phone bleeped at me.

Expecting it to be Sejin with some form of ranting email, I was pleasantly surprised to discover it was a variety show producer I had been trying to get a meeting with. I opened the message and quickly read it.

The early night was not happening. Ryu Mindo had agreed to meet this evening to discuss the possibility of H3RO appearing on his show. He wasn't available until after ten, it was going to be a late meeting, which at least meant I would be able to have a nap first.

I happily tapped back a confirmation, requesting he let me know where he wanted to meet, then slipped my phone back into my pocket. If I wanted that nap, we needed to leave. I hurried over to where Tae, Nate, and Kyun were still working. Even though we had called it a wrap, Kyun had insisted that the two go over the steps for their routine again.

"Can you continue this back at the dorm?" I asked, then stopped as another dizzy spell hit me.

"Holly?" Nate said, alarmed, jumping to my side.

I tried to wave him away. "I'm fine."

"You're bleeding," Tae declared, appearing in front of me.

"Huh?" He pointed at my nose, and my hand shot up. When I pulled my fingers away, there was indeed blood. "Ah, crap," I muttered, trying to find a tissue in my pocket.

Kyun thrust one at me, and I took it off him, putting it to my nose. "Tilt your head back," Nate instructed me.

"No, lean forward," Tae said. "It's best to lean forward."

"Guys," I sighed, pinching the bridge of my nose with the other hand. "It's just a nosebleed."

"We should take you to the hospital," Tae said.

I rolled my eyes at him. "Tae, it's a *nosebleed*. That's it. I've just been busy. This doesn't require a visit to the hospital. It will stop soon."

"I'm with Tae on this," Nate agreed.

"It's a nosebleed," I snapped, pulling the tissue away. "Look, it's stopped already." I didn't mean to snap at him, but I wasn't used to all this fuss, especially not over something as trivial as a nosebleed. I just wanted to get home and clean up properly.

"Let's go," Tae said, quietly. I shot him a look.

"Back to the dorm," he clarified.

I took a step towards the minibus, then faltered as another dizzy spell hit me. The next thing I knew, Nate had ducked down in front of me. "Nate, I'm fine," I insisted. I really didn't want to be the girl who needed carrying because of a stupid nosebleed.

"Let him," Tae all but growled at me.

I sighed, but complied, allowing him to carry me the short distance back to the minibus. "What's the matter with Holly?" Jun cried, jumping out of the bus.

"I had a nosebleed," I responded, still mortified.

"You're really pale," Minhyuk informed me, studying my face as Nate set me down.

"Let's not make this a bigger deal than it is," I told him. "It's a nosebleed."

"You look like you're going to pass out," Dante told me, bluntly.

I rolled my eyes. "You guys have watched way too many dramas," I informed them, my hands on my hips. "Let's just get home so I can shower and eat."

"You need to have some sleep," Tae told me.

I nodded my agreement. "I have every intention of having a nap too."

"A nap?" Tae repeated.

"I have a meeting tonight."

"Reschedule it."

"Not a chance," I scoffed. "I've been trying to book this for weeks and I know if I reschedule it, I will lose this opportunity."

"Reschedule it," he repeated, more forcefully.

I cocked my head. "No," I said. I was vaguely aware of the looks the other members were sharing. I had a feeling not very many people said no to Tae. "You may be H3RO's leader, but I'm your manager. This meeting is for you guys. I will be fine after a nap and something to eat."

Tae narrowed his eyes at me, then he glanced at Dante and nodded his chin at him. I half turned to Dante, but before I could face him, his hand had shot into my pocket, and something was tossed through the air to Tae. The minibus keys.

"I will walk to this meeting if I have to," I yelled. When all six of them jumped, guilt flooded me. Then the dizziness hit me again. I toppled towards the floor of the minibus, my hands shooting out to catch myself, but Dante got in there first. He helped me into a sitting positing with my feet on the ground outside. "I'm fine," I mumbled, not really feeling it.

"Uh-huh," he said, his tone saying he believed anything but.

A can of Pepsi was thrust at me. "Drink something sugary," instructed Minhyuk, popping the tab for me.

I took it, taking small sips. The effect was almost instant.

"What have you had to eat today?" Minhyuk asked.

I closed my eyes, trying to think. "I just had a bar of chocolate."

"And?" Nate pressed. When there was no answer, he turned to the others. "What's the last anyone saw her eat?"

"A banana at lunch," Jun responded.

"Porridge last night, I think," Kyun added, quietly.

I nodded. "That sounds right."

"I'm ordering food when we get back," Tae decided. "I'm also driving."

I sucked in a breath but nodded. I was tired and still dizzy. Much as I didn't want to show the weakness, it was safer not to drive, for all of us. "OK." With Nate's help, because I was still shaky, I climbed into the back of the minibus. The others piled in after me. "Are you awake enough to drive?" I asked Tae as an afterthought. "You've been working harder than I have."

"I'm not the one passing out."

"I didn't pass out," I grumbled.

Beside me, Nate lifted his arm to wrap around my shoulder, and pulled me against him. "Tae knows better than that," he assured me. "So, just relax. We're a couple of hours from the dorm. Have a nap."

I didn't have the energy to fight them. Instead, I closed my eyes, got comfortable against Nate, and went to sleep.

제16 장

H3RO

Badman

I was fussed over from the moment I left the
minibus until I could finally take my shower. I'd
woken when we arrived at the dorm and Minhyuk
opened the minibus door. Nate had tried to persuade
me to let him carry me up, but I refused. The nap had
done me the world of good.

Inside, I had been ushered to the couch where
Dante had pulled me down next to him, then used
himself as a pillow. "Dante," I sighed, as he gently
pushed my head down.

"Hush, and sleep some more while Minhyuk
cooks," he had insisted. Tae had appeared shortly after
with a warm, damp cloth to wipe the blood away from
under my nose.

Honestly, I wasn't sure why I couldn't go sleep in
my own bed, but I liked how Dante felt under me. His
hands were playing with my hair, and it felt soothing. I
soon fell asleep again. The next time I awoke, it was to
Jun gently shaking my shoulders.

"Noona, wake up," he muttered by my ear.

I sat up, yawning. "*Noona?*" I didn't have any objection to him calling me that: I was older than him, and it was the word a younger male could use to an older female. It was just a little unexpected.

Jun merely wiggled his eyebrows at me.

Nate had led me over to the table, while Minhyuk had placed a large bowl of bibimbap in front of me. Every so often, one of them would lean over and add something from a side dish to my bowl. I had devoured it while everyone watched. That was a little bit weird, but somehow, it was also comforting. I was finding myself growing ever more attached to these guys.

Finally, I pushed the bowl back, full. "Minhyuk-*ah*, that was delicious." I let out a satisfied sigh as I glanced at the clock on the wall. "I need a shower," I said, then gave Dante a pointed look. "That means you can't come in."

"Shame," Dante muttered under his breath.

I got up and went into my room. When I exited, carrying my shower things, I nearly walked into Tae and Nate who were waiting outside with their arms crossed. "Are you going to stop me showering?" I asked.

"No, but I want to stop you going to this meeting after."

I shook my head. "Tae, you have all looked after me and I feel so much better now. This meeting is really important. You're not going to stop me from going."

"Then I'm going with you," Nate shrugged.

"You don't need to do that."

"I am going with you," Nate repeated, firmly. "Tae has to get the song finished tonight, so I am going with you in his place. And I am driving."

"Then we need to leave in an hour," I said as I

slipped past them into the bathroom. I decided it was best to pick my battles. Besides it would be nice to have some company.

I showered quickly, then ducked back into my room to find something appropriate to wear. My dresses were either very office orientated, or summery. It was warm out, despite the rain, and the location I had been sent was a private room in a club in Hongdae.

In the end, I settled on a little black dress. It had a bodycon fit with a sweetheart neckline. I was hoping for understated, yet both club and meeting suitable. I put my heels on, then gathered my things together, putting them in my handbag. When I walked into the living room, Nate was already waiting for me, wearing dark jeans and a smart shirt.

I was also greeted by a low whistle from Jun. I turned to look at him, only to discover the stare he was giving me clearly said he wanted to take me out of the dress. I cleared my throat and turned back to Nate. "We should go."

Short of asking for the keys, and then where we were headed, the drive was spent in silence. We'd taken the Range Rover, and I settled back into the leather seats. I suspected he thought I might fall asleep again, but I was awake for now. A thrum of nervous energy running through me was keeping me going. I really wanted to get H3RO on this show.

When we pulled up, a short distance from the venue, Nate finally turned to me. "What is this meeting?"

"It's with the producer of 'Good morning K-Pop'," I told him, watching as his eyebrows disappeared under his fringe. "Exactly," I nodded.

"JongB said Onyx got good exposure on there," he said, quietly.

"Exactly," I repeated. "Now do you see why I was so insistent on coming?" At his nod, I sighed. "I wish you would trust me a little more. I really do want the best for H3RO." I gave him a sad smile, then slid out of the car with as much grace as I could manage in the short dress and heels.

I started walking towards the club, when Nate caught up with me, grabbing my wrist. "Holly, I do trust you when it comes to H3RO," he told me, a solemn look in his dark eyes.

"But?" I asked, waiting for the exception.

"It's you I'm uncertain about."

I faltered. I wasn't expecting that.

"That's not what I mean," he sighed, and rubbed at the back of his neck.

"Then what do you mean?" I asked, surprised at how hurt that made me feel.

He glanced down the street, frowning, like he was trying to think of the words to say. "I know you want the best for us, and you're doing all you can to look out for us, but I'm not sure you're doing the same for yourself," he finally told me.

"Of course I want what's best for me! If H3RO succeeds, *I* succeed!" I said, indignantly.

"You've not had much sleep recently," he told me.

"Neither have you," I pointed out. "At least I made it to bed while you pulled all-nighters in the dance studio."

"*I* don't look like I'm going to faint all the time," he shot back at me.

I opened my mouth for a retort, then stopped myself, shaking my head at him. This was going to go around in circles. "We are going to be late," I told him, instead. I pulled my wrist free then walked off to the club. I could sense Nate was just behind me, so I didn't turn to check.

At the door, I told the doorman Ryu Mindo was expecting us and a woman appeared to take us through into the back area where the private rooms were. I'd never been to a club like this before. I'd never been to a nightclub in Seoul, for that matter, but this was still a lot more upmarket than I was expecting. Something about a backroom made me feel like it would be seedy.

Inside, I was greeted by Ryu Mindo, who seemed a little surprised to see Nate with me but offered us a seat behind the small table. It was an odd set up. The little room had a round table at one end, and the seats, more like a bench, curved around so that we had to sit beside each other, rather than opposite.

Nate slid in first, and I followed. I was surprised then when Ryu Mindo chose to follow me, rather than sit beside Nate. "Forgive me, but I'm a little deaf in the other ear," he apologized as I ushered Nate around so we would have some more room. A woman came in shortly afterwards with a bottle of wine, pouring us each a glass.

Ryu Mindo was about the same age as Sejin, although a little shorter and a lot skinnier. He was a lot more charming, and honest. It was quite refreshing. "I must admit, I'm more up to date on the groups that have had comebacks in the last year," he told us. "I had to look H3RO up. A few on my team even thought you'd already disbanded."

"That's why I want H3RO on 'Good Morning K-Pop'," I told him. "It's such a well-known show in Asia and gathering a lot of attention internationally. I've yet to see an episode where I haven't laughed with the guests as they chatted with the hosts, and the challenges are always entertaining."

"You've done your homework," he said, smiling with approval. He leaned over and patted my thigh. "I approve of that."

I wasn't sure I approved of him touching me, but it was brief, and although he was a few years older than me, felt more fatherly than skeevy. I caught a growl from Nate and turned to him, shooting him a look. "Of course," I said, turning back to Ryu Mindo. "And Nate was telling me before he had heard wonderful things from when Onyx had been on the show."

"Ah, yes, your hoobaes," Ryu Mindo nodded. "They were a pleasure to have on the show. That Jiwon shows a great talent at variety shows already."

"I think, given a chance, you'll feel the same about H3RO," I said.

"And how do you feel about it?" Ryu Mindo addressed Nate.

"I think it will be good," Nate said, shortly.

I turned and shot him a look. That was not the way to appeal to this guy, and I knew full well that Nate knew that too. "Forgive him," I said, with a smile, to Ryu Mindo. "He does a lot better with a camera on him."

"I'm sure," the executive muttered. I reached for the glass of wine and took a sip, trying to work out a way to get around that. "I must say, I'm not sure why you're not in front of the camera."

I had to work hard not to choke on my drink. "Nobody should ever put me in front of a camera," I told him. "It would be the reverse of what you see here."

Ryu Mindo chuckled. "I'm not sure that is the case. But I like you. I think we can fit you in our schedule." He leaned around me to look at Nate. "I think it's time for us to talk business."

Nate glared back at him.

Trying to be as subtle as possible, I swiped at Nate's thigh. "Why don't you wait outside," I suggested. "This is the boring part."

Nate stared at me.

I stared back.

Then, with another low growl, he slid out from behind the table. "I'll be *just* outside the door," he told me, in English, fixing me a pointed look.

I waited for him to leave, before turning to the producer with an apologetic smile. "Please forgive him. He comes across as quite moody, but he's not really. We've both just come back from two days of filming their music video, so we're a little tired."

"You look like you had a wonderful beauty sleep," Ryu Mindo informed me.

That was generous. "The single will be released next week. When do you think you could fit us on?"

"I suppose that depends on you," Ryu Mindo responded.

I grinned. "For 'Good Morning K-Pop', I am prepared to move anything in our schedule around."

"That's not what I meant," he told me, scooting closer to me. The hair on the back of my neck shot up. "I have the power to get H3RO on the show, and every other show on the network." His hand settled on my leg, just below the bottom of my skirt.

For a full ten seconds, I started at my wine glass. I knew exactly what he was insinuating. I wasn't stupid. In the back of my mind, I had almost been expecting this since the first time he touched my leg. Even Nate had seen it coming.

The question was, how far was I prepared to go for H3RO.

The hand slid higher, under the skirt.

Not that far.

"H3RO and I are quite prepared to work with you to fit into your schedule," I said, surprising myself at how calmly I said those words. "You have my email, and my phone number. If you'd like to check your scheduling and let me know if anything fits in, I would appreciate that," I told him, before sliding out from behind the table.

"Do you know what you're doing right now?" he asked me.

I gave him a bright smile. "It was a pleasure to meet you."

With my head held high, I turned and walked out of the room. Nate was just down the corridor, leaning against the wall, one foot up, his arms crossed as he glowered at the floor. He looked up and saw me, eyeing me cautiously.

"I think that went well," I told him, forcing myself to keep the calm persona and positive attitude.

The caution changed to suspicion. "You do?"

"I hope to hear from him soon," I said, brightly. Technically, it wasn't a lie. I did hope to hear from him. I just had a feeling that phone call or email would never come. I gave Nate another smile. "Are you ready to head back, or would you like to stay a little while longer?"

Nate didn't say anything. Instead, he turned and walked off.

I took a moment to let out a long, shuddering breath, before straightening my back and following him.

The car ride was just as silent as it had been on the way to Hongdae. I spent the entire ride staring out of the window, unable to look over at Nate. I was starting to doubt my decision somewhere over the River Han, and by the time we had arrived back at the dorm, I was contemplating calling Ryu Mindo to see if there was any chance of another meeting.

It was past midnight when I typed the code into the door. I pushed it open, established that the lights were off, and therefore everyone else had had the sense to have an early night, when Nate grabbed my wrist. I released the door, managing to keep it from slamming shut with my foot, before I was pulled back to the elevator.

It hadn't moved since we had gotten in it, and Nate pulled me inside. "What are you doing?" I demanded as he hammered at the roof button. He ignored me and glowered stonily at his own reflection in the elevator door.

With an aggravated grunt, I pulled my wrist free and folded my arms in a cold silence. He was so infuriating sometimes. The doors pinged open and I stormed out, flinging my purse onto the cushions, before continuing to the far end of the rooftop.

It was cold out here now, a cool breeze whipping around the edge of the building. I folded my arms—

partly to try to keep warm, and partly to show my annoyance at Nate's behavior.

"Are you going to tell me what you did in there?" he demanded from behind me.

My fingernails dug into my bare skin as I whirled around to glower at him. "What I did?" I repeated. "I did the best I could to make sure you and the other members of H3RO have the best shot at this comeback."

Nate's mouth fell open. "What?"

The wind whipped my hair around my face, but I didn't bother to try to stop it. Instead I lowered my head and hid behind it. "And it still wasn't good enough," I mumbled, miserable.

Nate stepped forward, grabbing at my elbows. When I looked up at him, he brushed the hair from my face and stared angrily at me. "You mean you slept with him and he still—"

"What? No!" I cried, pulling free from him. "I was barely in there for a couple of minutes." I shook my head and stared past him at the sky. "That's the point, Nate: I didn't do anything with him. I just walked out of there."

Nate stepped into my line of sight, brushing my hair back again. The anger had been replaced with horror. "Then why are you so upset?"

"Because I've messed up H3RO's chances," I cried, before bursting into tears. There. I had said it aloud. "H3RO won't make it onto 'Good Morning, K-Pop', and from the sounds of things, none of the network's other shows."

"Woah!" Nate said, aghast. "Woah, woah, woah." He stepped forward, then his hands were under my chin, gently forcing it up so I had no choice but to look at him. "Holly, no. I—*we*—would never want you to do that for us. That's not how we would want this to work, ever. I can't even believe you'd think we expect that of you."

"You don't understand, Nate. Lee Woojin is my father. Lee Sejin is my brother. He made me your manager because he expects us both to fail. I don't want to disband you, but he does, and he wants to get me out of there too. I don't even care about me, but I can't let him disband you guys. I love you guys too much for that to happen, and I refuse to let him take out his pathetic family issues on H3RO." Tears streamed down my face as Nate stared down at me, unblinking, unmoving. "I *have* to get this right. I even expected that to happen when I walked in there, and I thought I could do what I needed to for you guys, but I couldn't, and I'm sorry."

Nate let go of me then, running his tongue over his lower lip as he continued to stare down at me.

I reached up to wipe the tears from my cheeks, even though the action was pointless. There was nothing stopping the tears at this point. "I think this is the point where I'm supposed to tell you I'll leave, but I'm not going to do that. I may have royally fucked us over tonight, but I'm going to find a way to fix this."

제17 장

H3R으

Under The Moonlight

Rage flashed through Nate's eyes as he grabbed at my wrist. He only just managed to prevent himself from dragging me across to the sheltered seating area, before he sat me down on one of the cushions. With a growl, he pulled one of the blankets off the back of the couch and draped it across my legs. Then he paced back and forth in front of me. Every so often he would stop, turn to me, and open his mouth. Instead of speaking, he'd shake his head and continue pacing again.

Finally, he walked over, standing over me. "I swear you are the only person who could think that sleeping with someone to get a job is acceptable."

I was on my feet, glaring at him in an instant. "Now hang on one minute," I snapped at him. "Under no circumstances do I think it's acceptable. The whole idea of it makes my skin crawl. Do you have any idea how angry it makes me when I read stories of actresses and singers who have admitted that they got jobs because they had no other choice but to sleep with someone?"

"Honestly, no," he admitted. "Because you were considering doing the same thing."

"That's why I couldn't do it," I told him. The tears were threatening to make an appearance again. "I'd promised myself that I'd never let myself get into that position—whatever job I was after—and then I get out here, go into a meeting where, within five minutes of being there, had the inkling that was the direction we were heading in, and I didn't leave. I'm mad with myself." I turned to kick one of the cushions, sending it flying into the middle of the roof. "I then stayed in that room, psyching myself up to do what I needed to, which makes me furious with myself."

"Holly," Nate sighed.

I shook my head. "And *then*, because I eventually did leave, even knowing that I was screwing things up, I'm also feeling disappointed in myself." The tears finally started falling again. "Then I get angry at being disappointed at myself, because that's the last thing I should be disappointed about, but at the same time I keep coming back to the fact that I've just stopped you getting on a number of variety shows."

Nate moved quickly, wrapping his arms around me, holding me tightly. "Holly, you did the right thing getting out of there. None of us would want to be on a show knowing that's how we got there."

"But—" my voice was muffled by his shoulder.

"We're about to release a really great song, with a brilliant video. We've had more done for us in the last couple of months than we've had in our entire career and that means more than a number one song." He pulled back and started wiping the tears from my cheeks. "If we get a number one, that's amazing, but it's not the best thing."

I stared up at him with watery eyes. "If you don't get a number one single, if you don't get a number one on two different charts, Lee Woojin and Lee Sejin will disband H3RO," I blurted out.

Nate nodded. "I figured."

My mouth slowly fell open. "You did?"

"I didn't realize it was two, but the way you've been so insistent about us getting to number one, and that we weren't being disbanded; I figured it would be something like that."

"Oh," I said, too dumbfounded to think of anything else to say.

"The thing is, and I speak for the others with this too, we would rather be disbanded than have you sleep with some scumbag executive to get us on shows. We'd rather take a single that barely charts than have that." Nate's hands slipped to my shoulders. "And if you're worried about your career, I'll look after you. I don't care if I have to move back to America, or if I have to work four part-time jobs to do so."

"I'm not worried about my job," I told him. "I never wanted it to start with."

"Then why are you still here?" he asked.

I shrugged. "I care about you guys too much."

Nate muttered something under his breath I didn't catch, and then he leaned down and kissed me. I resisted, starting to push back, but he kissed me harder. *To hell with it.* I wanted this too.

I reached out and grabbed at his shirt, clutching it between my fists. I tugged gently, pulling him back with me until the backs of my legs hit the edge of the couch.

I kicked my shoes off, losing three inches in height. Nate pulled back but I hung onto his shirt as he looked at me questioningly.

It was four in the morning. It was cold and we were in a rooftop garden which, although not directly overlooked, was barely sheltered from the surrounding buildings. So, naturally, I did the single craziest thing I'd ever done until that point. I let go of Nate so I could grab the bottom of my dress, then pulled it up over my head so I was standing there in just my bra and panties.

Nate stood there, staring. When I was starting to doubt what I was doing, and shivering, Nate finally sprung into life. I reached over, cold fingers fumbling to help unbutton his shirt as his mouth sought out mine again. As his tongue teased mine, I finally got the shirt off him.

Feeling his bare chest under my fingers, I pulled away so I could marvel at his torso. "Fuck me," I hissed, drinking him in.

"Yes, please," he responded in a low, husky whisper as I ran my hands over his muscles.

My hands moved lower, finding his belt. I made short work of it as Nate kicked off his own shoes, and then we were both standing on a rooftop in nothing but our underwear. Nate's hand slid around my back as he lowered me onto the oversized couch. The cotton cushions were cold and slightly damp beneath me.

Nate lowered himself over me, his mouth finding mine once more, kissing me like he had all the time in the world. I had no idea how he could be so calm when I could feel his erection rubbing up against me sending wicked sensations coursing through me.

Finally, after an eternity of teasing me, one of his

hands slipped under me, unclasping my bra. In an expert movement, it was gone. He pulled himself up on one arm to look down at me as the breeze skimmed over the top of my breasts. His eyes darkened, and then his lips fastened around one of my nipples. I gasped, arching up into him as his tongue continued to play with me.

My hands went to his head twisting into his golden-brown hair. He sucked harder, and when I started trying to rub against him to relieve the ache between my own legs, he switched his attention to the other nipple, repositioning his body out of my reach. "Nate!" I gasped, somewhere between a whine and a plea.

With his lips still teasing my nipple, he looked up at me, his eyes silently defying me. The hell with that. Let's see how he liked it. I pushed him off me, rolling him onto his back. Nate, tilted his head, bringing himself up on his elbows, but I shook my head and pushed him back down as I eased myself over him.

Before he could say anything, I was kissing him again. Slowly, my mouth left his and I started trailing kisses down his neck, pausing only to nip at his collar bone, which I'd been dying to do since the first shoot. Finally satisfied, and maybe leaving behind a mark or two as Nate had grunted his enjoyment, I moved downwards, enjoying the feeling of my breasts moving along his torso.

I paused briefly at his nipples changing the kisses to licks, then, when he moaned, I continued south, following the outline of that v-shaped muscle which disappeared under the top of his boxers.

"Holly," he grunted. I ignored him, and tugged at

his boxers, freeing him from the confines. He helped me, lifting his body, so I could pull his underwear off him completely. Then he was completely naked. I stepped back off the bed and stared down at him, so focused on his glorious naked form, that I completely forgot that I was on a rooftop, almost naked myself. "Holly?" He propped himself back up on his elbows to watch me.

I traced my eyes lazily up his body, committing every line and curve to memory, before finally meeting his gaze. "Just admiring the view," I told him.

"It's pretty spectacular from this angle too," he responded cheekily.

I grinned, then slowly sank to my knees as he continued to watch me. I wrapped my hand around him, smiling to myself as he groaned again, then leaned forward to take him in my mouth. He hissed but pushed himself further upwards. His hands fell into my hair, but he allowed me to stay in control.

After just a few strokes his hands suddenly reached under my arms and he pulled me up. "Spoilsport," I grunted at him, before he was kissing me again. Our bodies flush against each other.

Gone were the lazy kisses to be replaced with fast, urgent kisses. "I need to be inside you," he murmured in my ear.

"No objections here," I said, before gasping as he sucked at a sensitive area on my throat.

He pulled away, running a hand through his hair. "Fuck!" he cursed. I stared at him in confusion. "I don't have anything with me."

"Purse," I said, pointing over at the item I had thrown so carelessly to the side earlier.

Nate lunged for it, handing it over. I reached in, pulling out a little foil packet. "I have no words," he said, plucking the condom from me. I had barely tossed the purse back to the side before he had started kissing me again, even more hungrily than before. He picked me up, then lay me back down on the cushions, somehow, in the process, removing the last remaining shred of clothing from my body.

His hand skimmed up my thighs, and I barely had time to register what he was doing before he dipped two fingers inside me. He pulled away, staring down at me under heavy eyelids. "Oh, god, Holly, you're so wet," he grunted as his fingers started moving in and out, curling inside me.

Words escaped me. Literally. I was mumbling something, but like hell I could remember what. His fingers had me completely lost in a blissful haze. I was so close to falling over the edge, and then his fingers stopped.

My mumbles turned into complaints, but they quickly quietened when I heard the foil packet being ripped open. A few moments later, his hands were back on me, this time, running up and down my inner thighs, gently spreading my legs wider. He moved up me, positioning his tip at my opening, before meeting my gaze. "I love you," he told me, before kissing me, and finally entering me.

The kiss blocked the cry that came to my lips from escaping into the air. My fingers dug into his back, as my body adjusted to him, then he began moving, as steady as his kisses. How he could stay so gentle was beyond my thought capability. He was getting me all worked up and keeping me on the brink. I groaned in frustration against his kiss and started moving myself more, attempting to find my own completion.

As if he got the message, his thrusts became harder and faster, to the point kissing wasn't possible anymore. Each movement was sending ripples of bliss through me. I clutched at him, moving with him, allowing him to enter me more deeply. I locked eyes with him: he was as close to orgasm as I was.

One last hard thrust was all it took, and my eyes rolled into the back of my head as I screamed out my pleasure. He continued thrusting, dragging my orgasm out, then, as I was beginning to find some semblance of conscious thought, he groaned in my ear from his own orgasm.

His movements slowed. Finally, he removed himself from my body and fell to the side, wrapping his muscular arms around me and drawing me to him. Although we were both still trying to catch our breath, he showered me in kisses, sucking at my neck and nipping at my ear. I clung to him as the occasional residual pulse of the orgasm had my toes curling and my legs twitching.

His kisses slowed, and he reached over, seeking out the blanket I had used the previous night I had been up here and draped it over us. I settled into the nook of his arm, using his bicep as a pillow. One of his legs swung over mine, while his other hand brushed out my hair in lazy motions. He didn't take his eyes off me the entire time and I felt like the center of his world.

We lay there like that for a while, until finally, the wind picked up and the chill was stronger than the heat of our bodies. "We should head inside," he murmured in my ear.

I didn't want to leave his arms, but the roof was cold, and although sated, I was exhausted. I wriggled out from under the blanket, regretting it instantly as the cold attacked my still sensitive skin.

I pulled the dress on in a hurry, scooping my underwear up and shoving it in my handbag. I had just picked up my shoes when Nate draped his shirt over my shoulders. He'd pulled his pants and shoes on. It was a good thing it was some unreasonable hour in the morning, and no one could see us.

We hurried inside and back down to the dorm. I pushed open the door and walked in, Nate right behind me. I stopped suddenly: Jun was in the kitchen, illuminated by the light from the fridge. "You two are back late," he said. He pulled a bottle of water out of the fridge and let the door swing shut.

"We stayed out a little longer," Nate agreed, calmly. "And now I'm going to bed." He leaned around me and placed a kiss on my cheek. Then, with a nod at Jun, like that was the most natural thing in the world, he walked down the hallway to his bedroom.

I felt like a rabbit caught in headlights—and the headlights were Jun's eyes. He stared at me, then glanced down the hallway as Nate's door closed behind him. Then his attention was on my purse, before flicking back up on me. Before I could offer any form of explanation, he walked up to me, slipped a hand behind my neck, and then kissed me. Unlike Nate, he went straight for my mouth, and when I gasped in surprise, didn't hesitate in deepening the kiss.

And so help me, I kissed him back.

Then, as quickly as he initiated it, he stepped back and started walking towards his own room.

"Goodnight, noona," he called softly over his shoulder.

I waited for his door to close before I bolted to my own room, slumping back against the door. What was I doing? Aside from going to hell?

I glanced down at my bag. My bra was hanging out of it. A quick glance at my reflection in the mirror and my post-sex hair left no doubt as to why Nate and I had returned so late. Jun had to have known. He was young, but he wasn't stupid.

So why had he kissed me?

제18 장

H3R오

Attention

Possibly because I was that exhausted, I passed out and didn't wake until my alarm went off only a few hours later. I lay in bed for a while, staring at the ceiling, wondering what I was going to do with my life ... my love life.

I had slept with Nate.

It had been amazing.

He had told me he loved me.

Then I had kissed Jun.

Technically, Nate and I hadn't had a conversation about exactly what Nate, and I were, which meant *technically*, I hadn't really cheated on him ...

And then back to Jun ... Maybe I was going crazy. I mean, at this point, it was possible, but I swear he knew about Tae ...

And crap, there was Tae in this weird equation.

I had a niggling feeling that Jun maybe knew about Tae? I was certain he knew about Nate too. Yet, despite this he'd kissed me.

I rolled over with a groan. Last night, that hadn't

bothered me, but now I had slept off what had to be poor judgement brought on by an orgasm, I was questioning my own morality. These were two guys in the same damn group—the same dorms. Nate and Jun even shared the same damn bedroom.

There was a special place in hell for people like me.

All of that was forgotten when my phone chimed at me. I picked it up, read the email, and then let out an excited scream. The next thing I knew, Tae and Dante were in my room. "What's wrong?" Tae demanded.

I leaped out of bed, brandishing the phone at them "You're going on 'Idol Play'!" I yelled.

Dante and Tae turned to give each other a high five. "I'm telling Jun," Dante declared, disappearing.

Tae looked at me in amazement. "Even Onyx hasn't been on 'Idol Play'," he said. Then, as if falling out of his trance, strode across the room, cupped my face and kissed me. "Thank you," he murmured. He turned, leaving the room as he sidestepped past Jun who had appeared. "You heard?" he asked.

Jun was studying Tae but nodded. "Amazing, isn't it?"

Tae grinned. "It's 'Idol Play'!" he exclaimed and then he hurried off.

Jun turned to look at me, tilting his head. I sucked in a deep breath as the excitement in me was extinguished. He'd seen Tae kiss me. "Jun," I started, trying to work out how to explain myself as he walked over.

Jun gave me a small smile, leaned over and kissed me. Then, he gave me a smirk and sauntered off.

Without realizing I was doing it, my fingers traced

over my lips. He knew, right? He had to know ... so what was that about? And why was he seemingly OK with it?

H3RꝎ

Over the next few days, I got a few more emails confirming appearances, including two from popular music shows. I never heard back from Ryu Mindo, but one of the variety shows was on the same network, so things hadn't been lost completely. Tae had finished the production of the song, and then Soomi called to say the music video was finished.

While the guys were back in the dance studio, nailing down another dance, I went back to my apartment, and apologized to Kate for stealing the 60-inch screen from the bedroom. She helped me load it into the Range Rover.

At the dorms, I ran in and found they had returned. Dante, Minhyuk, Nate and Jun were in the kitchen. Minhyuk was busy making dim sum while the others watched on. "Could I borrow one of you?" I asked, sheepishly.

"Sure," Dante shrugged. "What for?"

"Your body," I shrugged.

Dante's eyes went wide, and he grinned. "I knew it." Before I knew what he was doing, he bounded down the hallway to the bedrooms.

"That's not what I meant," I called after him with a sigh as he disappeared.

Dante stuck his head out of the door. "Huh?"

"The car," I said, rolling my eyes. "I need help carrying something up."

Dante pulled a face then slowly made his way back to the kitchen, dragging his heels. "I think I preferred my suggestion," he said, disappointed, before disappearing out of the dorm.

"Well, you know I'm in," Nate declared, following after him.

I sighed again, then followed. They'd already claimed the elevator by the time I arrived. They didn't even know where they were supposed to be going. I jabbed at the button as Jun appeared next to me, leaning against the wall.

"I only needed one extra pair of arms," I told him. "You can go back to watching Minhyuk."

"I would much rather watch you," he said.

I arched an eyebrow at him. "Smooth."

"Yeah, OK, not my finest," he admitted as the elevator arrived. He followed me in, standing in front of me. "But now I get you all to myself for thirty seconds." One hand came to rest on the elevator beside my head, as his body pushed mine backwards. His lips claimed mine, as his other hand cupped between my legs.

And then the elevator called the parking level and he stepped back to exit the lift, acting like nothing had happened. I glared at the back of his head. In the shortest elevator ride known to man, that little bastard had managed to work me up. I walked out and clipped the back of his head as I joined him, Dante and Nate.

Nate arched an eyebrow. "What is that about?"

"He knows," I growled, darkly, while Jun chuckled to himself, muttering something that sounded like *worth it* under his breath. I ignored him, led them over to the car and popped the trunk. "I only needed one of you to give me a hand with this."

"Holy shit, Holly!" Dante exclaimed.

"What's this for?" Jun asked.

I shrugged. "I really wanted a movie night," I told them. "I figured you'd all be tired from dancing all day and could do with a night off. Or a few hours at least. And your television is tiny."

Dante and Nate pulled the television out of the back and the four of us headed back up. Minhyuk's mouth fell open as we walked in. "Where did you steal that from?"

"Call it a gift from Lee Woojin," I told him.

The television was too big for the existing unit, so I got the guys to take the chest of drawers from my bedroom and use that. The noise drew Tae and Kyun from their bedroom. "What is that?" Tae asked suspiciously.

"A television, hyung," Jun stated, cheekily. That earned him a clip around the back of the head as Tae turned to me for an explanation.

"Movie night tonight." I looked between him and Kyun. They were both hot and sweaty. "Unless you two have plans?" I didn't care what they got up to, that was their business. Although I was now slightly confused as to why Tae had kissed me.

"We were practicing," Kyun snapped at me.

I held my hands up. "I think Minhyuk's nearly finished preparing the dim sum, so if you two want to clean up, we can all settle in for the night." I walked past them to my bedroom. I'd left the Apple TV box in there and I would need it to project the music video to the television.

I turned around, box in hand, finding Tae leaning in the doorway, fixing me a stern look. "There is nothing going on between Kyun and I," he informed me.

"Even if there was, it would be none of my business," I shrugged.

"It is your business," he corrected me. "And there's nothing there. It's just Kyun …" he trailed off.

"Tae," I said, holding my hand up. "It's really not my business."

I ducked past him and hurried down to the living room, tossing Dante the box which he plugged in.

A while later, the dining table had been moved in front of the two couches like a coffee table and was covered in the food Minhyuk had made. I was impressed. He really was a good chef.

The two couches were three seaters each, but I found myself wedged between Jun and Dante, with Minhyuk on the far side. Considering Tae was on the other couch with Kyun, and Nate, who had decided to use my legs as a back rest, choosing to sit on the floor, I wasn't sure if there was a need for us all to be squished together, but I was comfortable.

When we'd finished eating, I pulled my iPad over. "What are we watching?" Kyun asked, gruffly. I didn't say anything. I just shared my screen and hit play.

Dante's face filled the screen and the room erupted into so much noise, I had to hit pause. Dante turned to me, grabbing my wrist. "Is this it?"

I nodded, but Jun leaped to his feet. "Wait!" he cried, running off to his room. He charged back, moments later with the camera from the cabin, and a tripod, setting them up next to the television. "Reaction video!" he cried, racing back to sit next to me. I started to stand, but Jun grabbed my hand. "Where are you going?" he demanded. On the other side, Dante, who still had my wrist, was tugging me down.

"Out of camera shot," I said, pointing at Jun's set up.

"Nonsense. You're our manager. You're allowed to be in the shot," Minhyuk pouted at me.

"And yet, we could have all of you in one shot, and I can use the zoom button," I said. "This is your moment. Enjoy it."

"You're a part of it too," said Tae.

It warmed my heart to hear that, and I flashed him a smile, but I still freed myself from Dante and Jun's grip. "I'll join in on the second viewing. You two get over there," I told Tae and Kyun. While I moved to the camera, they relocated. "OK, someone hit play."

The music video was nearly five minutes long. The only way I knew who was on the screen was from the reactions. Tempted as I was to peek, I wanted to be able to watch it properly, and I was rather enjoying seeing how excited the guys were. They were quick to compliment each other, and their facial expressions ranged from awe and amazement to pure pride at each other.

The video finished and the room erupted into a round of applause and cheers. "Soomi did a decent job then?" I asked, setting the camera down.

Dante jumped up, leaping over the table, sending things flying. While the others laughed, clearing up the mess, Dante scooped me up in his arms. "What are you doing?" I squealed.

"You are watching it with us now!" He carried me back over to the couch and sat down, keeping his arms clamped around me to keep me from moving out of his lap. That didn't stop me wriggling as I tried to move back to my original position. "You might not want to move around so much," he murmured in my ear.

I froze, wondering what he meant, and then I felt him. I stilled, wondering how much I wanted to torture him. Then I became aware of Jun sat next to me, watching us like he knew, and I pushed the idea quickly from my head, biting at my lip.

"Are you ready?" Minhyuk cried, hitting play before I could say yes.

Dante's face once again filled the screen.

I wanted to watch it again, and again, with an option to play it at half speed so I could take it all in. I was also going to make sure Soomi was well rewarded. She was going to be directing and producing the other two videos. If I had any power at Atlantis, I was also going to suggest that she be used for other artists too.

I lost myself in the story of the video. As Soomi had described, she'd gray washed the story part, so it looked dismal and bleak. With the rain pouring down in so many of the shots, the situation looked terrible, in a good way.

H3RO were being chased by an unknown group of people for the most part. They started off in a group, outside by the river. Part way through, they split up into three groups. There was a part where Jun had fallen over, twisting his ankle, and Nate had gone back to pull him onto his back. Jun's look of pain looked so realistic, I had to remind myself he was only acting.

Dante and Kyun got cornered at one point, and the two of them had to battle their way out of capture. When Dante got a kick to the chest, sending him flying, my hands gripped at the arms wrapped around me. The shot had been done so that Dante had barely been touched—all rigged up on strings and had involved a safety mat—but that didn't stop me wincing. Then, when Kyun got punched in the face, I bit my lip so hard, I could taste blood.

By the end, the six of them had all met back up in the parking lot, running up to the roof. There was a look of terror on Jun's face, which had me reaching for his hand. He squeezed it back, rubbing his thumb over the back of my hand in reassurance. He was the reason they were being chased—that was all they had been told. Instead of being captured, he turned and leaped off the side of the building. My hand, which wasn't being held onto by Jun, clutched at my chest.

All the while, there were groups shots of them dancing. Some in the rain, some in an abandoned room, both in glorious color. Especially the solo shots of Minhyuk dancing with the rain pouring down on him. It was beautiful.

It was ridiculous how invested I had gotten in a five-minute video. I hadn't seen any of it, so while my body was tense for most of it, it only eased up for the last shot: a drone panning over Tae, Dante, Nate, Minhyuk and Kyun as they were led away bound in rope. The drone continued, over the side of the parking lot to look at the ground below. Instead of being greeted by an image of Jun, there was nothing.

The video stopped and I looked around the room, so proud of them. We'd been given next to no budget, had to rely solely on help from so many people, and yet they had put everything into this video, and it showed. They'd also done so much of it—the song and the choreography—by themselves. I was so proud of them.

"You guys liked it, right?" I asked, suddenly realizing I'd never asked them that.

"I think I speak for everyone when I say that is the best thing we've done," Tae said, as five heads nodded in agreement. "I'm actually glad we didn't get the type of budget Onyx sees, because this was low budget and it was incredible. We'd have been lost in special effects otherwise."

"Even if we don't get a number one from this, I don't think we could do any better," Minhyuk agreed.

That was true. "If you don't get a number one single from this, it's because Atlantis Entertainment let you down, not because of anything you guys did or didn't do," I told them, firmly. That was also true. As was the fact that I was part of Atlantis Entertainment. I would hold just as much responsibility as the company.

I just hoped Sejin would see how hard they worked and not be a complete dick this time.

For some reason, the mood in the room had dropped a little, and, given how amazing the music video had been, I was desperate to bring it back up. I gave the room a bright smile. "I have something else for you."

Minhyuk cocked his head, while Jun's eyes went wide in anticipation. "What?" Dante asked.

"Tonight, your fandom has earned a name and color." Six sets of eyes stared at me, but I pointed at the television. In an almost eerie movement, they simultaneously turn their attention back to the screen. I closed the video player and pulled open the document.

"Treasure," Tae read aloud. "And purple."

"Technically, that's pantone number 2587C," I said. When the six of them just stared at me, I shifted awkwardly. Maybe I should have just left things as they were. "Is it that bad?"

"We have a fandom name?" Minhyuk asked in disbelief.

I nodded.

"In six years, we've never had one," Dante was muttering.

"Noona, it's perfect," Jun exclaimed, wrapping his arms around me in excitement. "H3RO and their Treasure. I love it!"

"He's right," Tae agreed.

"For once," Dante added with a frown.

제19 장

H3RO

Lies

The night of the release of the music video, I was a wreck, although I was trying desperately hard not to show it. We had released all the teaser images and they had been well received. There had been two teaser clips for the video: the first of the group dancing, the second of the group running. I had been amazed at how well they had been clocking up views on YouTube alone.

The video and the single were to go live at exactly one-minute past midnight. Until then, I was pacing back and forth in my room, constantly going back to check I'd set everything up correctly.

By five minutes to midnight, I thought I was either going to throw up or pass out. I had never been as nervous about anything in my life. Not even when I had been forced to pack my bags and move out to Seoul to work for a father I knew nothing about.

I sucked in a few deep breaths, and then left the safety of my room, hoping my acting skills were half way as decent as Dante and Kyun's had been. The guys were all sitting around in the living room. I almost laughed in relief to see them. They were trying so hard to act casual and nonplussed that they all looked awkward. "We're nearly there, guys," I declared, syncing the iPad up to the television.

It was already loaded with the Atlantis Entertainment YouTube channel. On the couch in front of me, Jun had the V-Live app open. Finally, on the table, the laptop had tabs for Instagram, Facebook, Weibo and Twitter, all with messages ready to go.

Because, of course, we were still taking care of all the marketing ourselves.

As soon as the clock changed to midnight, I hit refresh repeatedly. On cue, at exactly one-minute past, the video appeared. When I refreshed again, and the views had jumped to eleven. I hit the button again, and a leap had been made.

30,078 views.

How was that even possible?

We all looked at each other in stunned silence. I hit refresh again, and we had broken *one hundred thousand* views.

The room erupted into chaos with the guys hugging each other while I stepped back and uttered a quiet prayer of thanks. In reality, the video streams were only a small part of what was counted in the charts, but hell, this was a good sign. People were at least watching the video.

The iPad was taken over by Jun who pressed play on the video. "Hey, it can't hurt, can it!" he declared, cranking up the volume. The next thing I knew, the six of them were dancing the routine. It occurred to me that I could probably take pictures or video of this, but I decided against it. They could keep this moment private.

Instead, I decided I would bring out my small treat. I chuckled to myself as I stuck my head in the refrigerator. Earlier, I had snuck a bottle of champagne in and hidden it in the bottom behind the beer that had remained untouched since we had returned from the cabin as everyone was watching their figures.

"What are you doing?" Nate asked, creeping up beside me.

I squealed and dropped the bottle as I leaped up. Nate's arms shot out to steady me. I lowered my head against his chest, trying to control my beating heart. His embrace tightened and a hand started stroking at the back of my head.

I breathed in his scent, having a flash back of the other night. Something rippled through me, and I pulled away, dropping down to the floor behind the small island, so I could pick up the, thankfully, unbroken bottle.

"I think I should hold off opening this for a while," I muttered to myself, still on the floor, as I tried to calm my hormones which had suddenly fired into action.

Nate crouched down beside me, so close, that if one of us were to say something, our lips would end up touching: it wouldn't take much for us to be kissing. Least of all my non-existent willpower. Before I could think about what I was doing, I did just that. Maybe it was the excitement, or the nerves, or maybe it was just the fact that I really was attracted to him.

Then I sensed someone behind Nate. I pulled away, just as Jun stepped around the side of the island. Nate looked over his shoulder, then turned back to me and kissed me once more before getting to his feet. He walked off with the bottle of champagne, leaving me once again feeling sheepish in front of Jun.

Jun walked over and offered out a hand. I took it. "Thank you," I muttered, not quite meeting his gaze. Realizing I could keep myself busy with something, I hurried over to the cupboard and started pulling out mismatched mugs. I hadn't thought about champagne flutes when I'd bought the champagne, and this dorm didn't have any.

"Here." Jun reached up behind me, standing so close, we were pressed up against each other. My hand hovered, frozen as he lowered the remaining cups, his hand constantly brushing mine, sending tingling feeling shooting down my arms. "My fingers are pretty talented, *remember.*" he whispered into my ear.

Then, like nothing had happened, he gathered up the mugs and sauntered over to the others. I stood there for a moment, clutching at the side. *Holy hell!* I didn't know if I wanted to murder him or get him to give me a reminder of how talented those fingers were.

OK, that's a lie: I knew exactly what option I wanted.

At 2 a.m., I ordered the group to bed. We had an appearance on Inkigayo, which had a relatively early roll call, and I wanted them all to have a good night's sleep before their first live comeback performance. That notion had me excited and terrified all over again. The view counts were continuing to go up, but this was also their first live performance in nearly fifteen months.

It was closer to three before the last bedroom door closed. I sank into the empty couch and rested my head in my hands. My body was running on adrenaline and I needed to burn it off before I would be able to sleep, though I wasn't convinced that was going to happen.

Cleaning. The room needed tidying up after our mini celebration. That would occupy me. I got up and began collecting the cups. "What are you doing?" Tae asked me, making me jump.

This time, I didn't drop anything. "Cleaning up," I replied with a shrug. I moved around to the sink and deposited them in the semi-full bowl.

"Can't sleep?"

I shook my head. "I'm too buzzed." I finally turned to face him. He was wearing a pair of basketball shorts and an oversized Supreme hoody. "That's not what you normally sleep in."

"I'm going to the store," he told me. "Want to come?"

"At this time of night?" He gave me a secret smile, then scooped up my hand. He led me out of the apartment and out onto the street, past the 7-11. "Which store are we going to?"

I hadn't explored much of the area, and the street he led me down was unfamiliar. We got to a busier road and waited to cross. Despite the hour, there was a fair amount of traffic. "Seriously, Tae. Where are we going?"

"It's a surprise," he muttered, stepping off the curb so he could face me.

"What are you doing, idiot?" I demanded, pulling him back up.

He moved straight away, and then we were toe-to-toe. He bent his head down and pressed his lips against my forehead. "You are incredible," he told me.

"Don't be giving me any credit for all the work you've been doing," I scoffed. "You wrote and co-produced an album. And don't get me started on that video. You—all of you—are the incredible ones."

"That's not what I'm talking about."

"The man's gone green," I muttered. Nate, Jun and Tae? I couldn't cope with this. I had no idea how, but I was going to have to choose one, and until I did, I really needed to behave myself. I was being selfish. The fact was, at the moment, I was doing all kinds of things with three guys I was insanely attracted to and I didn't want to stop, especially when they were blissfully unaware of what I was doing.

Or at least Tae and Nate were. I was positive Jun knew. Though that wasn't stopping him. "Tae," I sighed, reaching up to rest a hand on his chest.

His hand wrapped around mine. "I owe you an apology."

I blinked up at him. Well, that was unexpected. "You do?"

He nodded, solemnly. "I have yet to make good on my promise."

"Promi ..." I trailed off, mid question. Tae had made one promise to me—to finish what he had started. "Oh, that's OK," I said, hurriedly. "I mean, we've all been busy, and I don't want to hold you to anything."

"I keep my promises, Holly," he assured me, his voice low and grumbly. "Especially when I want to."

I swallowed, taken aback by the intensity in his eyes as he said that. Because he was usually so serious, Tae's gaze was intense to start with. This one was telling me the only thing stopping him from delivering on that promise right there was the fact we were standing on the side of the street. Oh, holy hell. I was screwed. He bent back to me, only this time, his mouth went directly to mine. *Completely screwed.*

His tongue teased at my lips while his hands settled on the small of my back. I closed my eyes, parted my lips, and his tongue delved in. I lost myself in the kiss; in him. I could feel the promise from him, and I was all set to collect.

Then a car horn blared, and he pulled away with a small smile. "Later." His hand sought mine again, and he led me across the road.

The store he took us to sold CDs. I hadn't even thought about the physical copies outside of the KpopKonneKt campaign. The idea of buying one from a store at this time of night, on release day, was as invigorating as watching the music video go live.

We hurried up and down the aisles, seeking it out. I couldn't see it. Tae shot me a questioning look, but I had no answer. "Maybe there's a new release section we missed. Wait here," I told him, thinking if he got spotted buying his own album, that would be all over the SNS.

I waited for the cashier to finish serving someone. "I'm looking for H3RO's new album."

He sighed. "Another one."

"Huh?"

He shrugged. "I've had so many people come in here tonight to buy that or pick up their pre-order, but I don't have any."

"It's sold out already?" I asked in excitement.

The excitement evaporated at the shake of the cashier's head. "It probably could have done, if any had been sent out to me."

"Huh?" I repeated, dumbly.

He shrugged again. "I called a few other stores. It seems the physical copy was never sent out today. I have to wait until tomorrow before I can contact the distributor, but if you want to be added to the waiting list, I will send out a mass email tomorrow when I have more information."

I zoned out, his voice deafened by confusion and horror. Had I fucked up? Again?

I moved away from the counter and plucked out my phone, logging onto the Atlantis Entertainment network. The server was down. "Is everything OK?" Tae asked from beneath his hood, appearing beside me.

"I had to sign a waiting list," I told him, vaguely. I looked over my shoulder and forced a smile. "I guess we should have had the foresight to pre-order."

"That sounds like good news to me," Tae beamed as he reached for my hand again.

It took everything I had not to cry as I smiled back at him. I hated lying, and yet that seemed to be all that I was doing lately.

H3RO

I hadn't slept all night. I had ended up with my iPad in front of me, constantly refreshing YouTube, watching the view number creep up. By sunrise, we'd hit half a million views. International fans really were incredible.

It wasn't the only thing the single was creeping up. Finally back in the States, Kate had sent a congratulatory screenshot of the iTunes and Billboard charts. We'd hit top ten in both.

Rather than watching H3RO's Inkigayo performance, I was trying to work out what had happened from side stage. I should have been enjoying the moment, buzzing at the fact that they were killing it and the whole audience knew the fan chant already.

The guys were killing it because, just before going on stage, they'd heard the news that they'd hit number one in the Gaon Digital chart. Their first number one. They were ecstatic, and I wanted to be too, but I wasn't.

Instead, I was fighting to keep from throwing up as my stomach churned. I hadn't eaten anything, and I wasn't sure there was anything to throw up, but that didn't stop the sick feeling in my stomach.

The server had just gone back online and I was staring at the form I'd submitted. I had put the right dates and figures, but it was still awaiting approval from Lee Sejin.

He was also ignoring my calls, text messages and emails. I seethed side stage, ready to leave there and then, march to Sejin's office, and throw him out of his window. How could he do that?

On stage, the charts were being announced. I didn't want to listen: I knew they weren't getting that number one. Inkigayo also needed physical copies.

As soon as it was announced that the top three places were held by Onyx, iKON and Twice, my phone burst into life. It was a text message from Sejin. **You'd best get to the office …** It wasn't even a question.

I darted backstage to our green room's bathroom and threw up. It was little more than stomach bile, and I didn't feel any better afterwards. Before H3RO could join me in there, I rinsed my mouth out and tried to fix my appearance, including trying to front the positive attitude they needed.

제20 장

H3R오

Nothing's Over

The drive back to the dorm was like torture for me. Despite the numerous text messages from Sejin—now he wanted me—I wasn't going to hurry the guys. They may not have gotten the Inkigayo win, but they were still thrilled about the Gaon win. They had held their heads high as 24K reperformed their song, and then stuck around to congratulate the other groups. They'd even received their own selection of complements and I wasn't going to do anything to wipe the smiles from their faces.

Not tonight.

My cheeks hurt from the smile I'd fixed on it.

"Noona, you promised meat!" Jun cried from the back of the minibus.

"I know I did," I responded, keeping the smile on my face. "But you guys need a shower, so go do that, and I will take us out later."

They all bounded out of the minibus and disappeared upstairs, chatting animatedly.

Finally alone, I let the smile fall from my face.

Feeling like a prisoner walking the green mile, I trudged to the Atlantis Entertainment building and went straight up to Sejin's office. I was about to go in when Tae appeared beside me. "Why are you here?" he asked, confused.

"You should head back to the dorm," I instructed him, ignoring his question. "You need to get that makeup off and cleanse your face."

He was still wearing what he'd performed in, from the eyeliner, right down to all performance clothes, complete with various pieces of jewelry. "Why are you here?" he asked again.

"I have a meeting with Lee Sejin," I shrugged. "Don't worry about it. You go back and enjoy this afternoon."

"You're acting strange."

The door opened and Sejin was standing there, glowering at me. "How much longer do you plan on making us wait?" he demanded. He then turned his attention to Tae, arching an eyebrow in amusement. "You might as well come in too."

"That's not necessary," I objected, hurriedly.

Tae shot me a questioning look but stepped past Sejin into his office.

"Please don't do this in front of him," I quietly begged Sejin.

He ignored me and marched into his office, joining his father on one of the hideous leather couches. He pointed to the one opposite. Tae sat as requested, bowing his head respectfully at the Chairman and Vice Chairman. I sat down beside him, but only because my legs had turned to jello and I had about four more seconds before they gave out on me.

"You got a number one," Sejin announced.

Tae nodded. "Yes, sir. Largely thanks to Holly."

"But it's only one number one," he continued.

"Their first number one!" I cried. "And it could have been two or more if the physical copies of the albums had been distributed on time."

"And did my sister explain to you what would happen if you only got one number one?" Sejin pressed, ignoring me.

Tae frowned, looking from Sejin to myself, then back at Sejin. "Your sister?"

Sejin pointed at me. "Holly. Didn't she tell you?"

I dropped my head, unable to look at Tae. I could feel the energy from him change. He moved away from me. "What would happen with a number one single?" he asked, carefully. I could feel his eyes burning into the side of my head.

"I was going to disband H3RO," Sejin explained, like the idea of disbanding them was as ordinary a decision as picking a side dish. "But I told her, that if you guys could get a number one on your comeback, I would let you guys keep your contracts."

"Then that's a good thing," Tae responded.

"If it were only that simple," Sejin tutted. "Holly decided one wasn't a big enough challenge and promised two."

"It wasn't like that!" I cried, finally turning to look at Tae. I wished I hadn't when all I saw was betrayal there. I turned to Sejin. "And we could have done it if we'd have had those album sales."

"H3RO didn't even rank in the top three on Inkigayo," Sejin told me, coldly. "Physical copies or not, they wouldn't have hit the Inkigayo number one, nor the Gaon Album chart."

"We got a number one!" I cried, pleading with him. "You can't disband them off the back of that!"

"You've already made that deal with me and failure on your part made the decision for me too," Sejin shrugged.

I couldn't stop the tears leaking from my eyes. I also couldn't bring myself to look at H3RO's leader, but I did. "I'm sorry," I told him, barely able to see him through the tears. Tae's stare had turned cold and foreign. It was like I no longer knew the person staring back at me, and I couldn't blame him. "I'm so, so, so sorry," I said again, reaching out for him.

Tae jerked out of the way, getting to his feet. "I'd best tell the others." His voice was unrecognizable too. Upset, hurt, disappointed.

In that moment, I knew there was nothing I could do to get Sejin to change his mind: it had been made up since before I had arrived. The only thing I could do now was give him something he wanted more …

Me.

My humiliation, and my share of the company.

Fuck it.

I had nothing to lose.

I dropped to my knees in front of Sejin. "Please," I begged him. "Please do not punish H3RO because of my failure. Please. I'll go back to America if you want me to, but please, please don't disband H3RO." I dropped my head into a kowtow. There was no shame anymore. I was prepared to do anything I needed to, to keep them together. "Please." At Sejin's feet, the only thing left for me to do was pray.

So, I did.

Then my miracle happened.

"Did anyone specify when this second number one was supposed to occur?" I looked up at Lee Woojin, but didn't dare breath, let alone say anything.

"Well, no, but—"

"There were no timelines agreed?" he pressed.

"No!" I suddenly cried.

Sejin shot me a murderous look. "We were discussing this comeback," he said, derisively.

"But, to be clear, there was nothing to specify that this comeback was required to have two number one singles?"

"Technically, no," Sejin whined, suddenly acting like he was a six-year-old. "But it was implied.

"As far as I see it, if the terms were not clearly specified, then the disbandment cannot be based upon this single number one. However, as a second number one was mentioned, I fully expect that the next comeback will have one."

I blinked up at him, trying to see my father through my tears. "Huh?"

"H3RO have survived this comeback. The next one is up to you."

I stared up at him, unable to move, sure that if I did, I was either going to faint or cry. Neither of which was appealing.

Then, behind me, a door slammed shut.

I turned. Tae had gone.

Tae!

I got to my feet and nodded my head at Lee Woojin. "Thank you," I told him, sincerely. And then I ran from the room as fast as I could, trying to find Tae.

H3RO may have survived Atlantis, but could they survive me?

To be continued …

… H3RO's story is not over yet!

If you've enjoyed what you've read so far, please, please leave a quick review on Amazon! They really help authors out and I (like H3Ro) would appreciate all the help given.

Sign up to Ji Soo's newsletter to receive release alerts, and keep tabs on the other groups at Atlantis Entertainment (did you know Bright Boys had recently debuted?):

Head to
https://sendfox.com/JSLee
to sign up

CHAPTER TITLES

The chapters in this book are all named after song titles:

1. *Hero* by Monsta X
2. *Boss* by NCT U
3. *Hey You* by 24K
4. *Playground* by U-KISS
5. *Really Really* by Winner
6. *War of Hormone* by BTS
7. *Devil* by Super Junior
8. *You Are* by GOT7
9. *Irresistible Lips* by BTOB
10. *Come Back When You Hear This Song* by 2pm
11. *Tell Me What to Do* by SHINee
12. *Can You Feel It?* by Pentagon
13. *What Am I To You?* by History
14. *Dress Up* by Boys Republic
15. *Gotta Go To Work* by Beast
16. *Badman* by B.A.P.
17. *Under the Moonlight* by VAV
18. *Attention* by UP10TION
19. *Lies* by Big Bang
20. *Nothing's Over* by Infinite

CHARACTER
BIOGRAPHIES

H3RO

Name: H3RO (헤로)
Fandom: Treasure
Colors: Purple
Debut: 2012-03-15

H3RO consists of 6 members:
Tae, Dante, Nate, Minhyuk, Kyun and Jun.

The group debuted on March 15th, 2012.

Stage Name: Tae (태)

Birth Name: Park Hyun-Tae (박현태)
Position: Leader, Vocalist
Birthday: March 1st
Age: 27
Zodiac sign: Pisces

Height: 182 cm
Weight: 62 kg
Blood Type: A

Tae facts:
He was born in: Incheon, South Korea
Family: Mother
If H3RO were a family, he would be the dad
Takes the role of leader very seriously
Protective of his group
Has a short temper
He shares a room with Kyun
Speaks Korean and Japanese

Stage Name: Dante (단테)

Birth Name: Guan Feng (关峰 / 풍관)
Position: Main vocals, visual
Birthday: June 24th
Age: 25
Zodiac sign: Cancer
Height: 183 cm
Weight: 72 kg
Blood Type: O

Dante facts:
He was born in: Hong Kong, Hong Kong
Family: father, mother
If H3RO were a family, he would be the rebellious son

The member who spends the most time in front of the mirror
He shares a room with Minhyuk
His favorite food is chicken
Speaks Chinese, Korean, and English
Sleeps naked

Stage Name: Minhyuk (민혁)

Birth Name: Kwon Min-Hyuk (권민혁)
Position: Rapper (high), dancer
Birthday: May 24th
Age: 24
Zodiac sign: Gemini
Height: 176 cm
Weight: 60 kg
Blood Type:

Minhyuk facts:
He was born in: Ulsan, South Korea
Family: father, mother
If H3RO were a family, he would be the mom
Loves cleaning
He shares a room with Dante
The mood maker of the group
Speaks Korean and Japanese

Stage Name: Nate (네이트)
Birth Name: Nathan Choi
Position: Dancer, rapper (low)
Birthday: May 11th
Age: 24
Zodiac sign: Taurus
Height: 178 cm
Weight: 58 kg
Blood Type: AB

Nate facts:
He was born in: San Francisco, USA
Family: father, mother
He shares a room with Jun
The peacemaker of the group
His favorite food is sushi
Speaks English and Korean
Is no good at chat-up lines

Stage Name: Kyun (균)

Birth Name: Ha Kyun-Gu (하균구)
Position: Vocals

Birthday: February 3rd
Age: 23
Zodiac sign: Aquarius
Height: 181 cm
Weight: 65 kg
Blood Type: B

Kyun facts:
He was born in: Incheon, South Korea
Family: Doesn't speak about them
He shares a room with Tae
Often reacts to uncomfortable situations with anger
Does not eat meat, but will eat fish
His favorite food is ramen

Stage Name: Jun (준)

Birth Name: Song Jun-Ki (송준기)
Position: Maknae, vocals
Birthday: February 18th
Age: 23
Zodiac sign: Aquarius
Height: 175 cm
Weight: 65 kg
Blood Type: AB

Jun facts:
He was born in Hwaseong, South Korea
Family: Father, mother

He shares a room with Nate
Enjoys photography
Hardest member to wake up
Can fall asleep anywhere
Pizza
Previously known as JunK

ACKNOWLEDGEMENTS

First and foremost, I need to thank you—you who is reading this. I had this crazy idea that there wasn't enough K-Pop fiction in books. Then I started to wonder if there was a reason for this and the self-doubt crept in. But I kept on writing, and you are the reason I finished, and the reason I will keep on building the Atlantis Empire.

After you, I owe so much thanks and gratitude to Cheryl Coffey, who isn't just my publisher, but is the person who allowed me to write. Literally. If it wasn't for Cheryl letting me use one of her Office licenses, I would be using Notepad. Aaaand, she's the one who converts everything to PDF for me too! She was also the one who put the idea in my head and brought the story to life. On top of that, she's the person who introduced me to Sarah and Leanne.

Sarah, thank you for being such a brilliant person! Sarah is the one who will send me pictures and gifs at all hours of the day to keep me motivated. Like Cheryl, I bounce my ideas off her, and she is able to give me clarity when I have too many ideas clouding the way. I mean, she's also part of the reason Atlantis is going to have such a big roster because THE IDEAS DON'T STOP! If this wasn't enough, she reads every first draft (sometimes incomplete first drafts) and reassures me when I'm having a crisis of confidence AND she gives the book its first edit. Usually in two days, which is a little intimidating because I cannot write a book in two days, but she's always waiting (im)patiently for the next one.

The other member of my Alpha team is Leanne. Leanne, as well as having that first sanity read, has been amazing of rounding out characters and helping with the details which seem small, but really aren't. She's also always being sent random shots of idols at stupid o'clock in the morning with the question of "who is this?" (because a girl has visual inspiration)!

Of course, a book isn't a book without a cover. For this amazing work of art, I have Natasha at Natasha Snow Designs to thank. I emailed her earlier in the year with a giant email of a request that included the question, "what do you know about K-Pop?". A short (who am I kidding, it wasn't short) PowerPoint presentation later, and I had received a response to thank me for introducing her to BTS. I have no regrets! When it came to the actual cover, she managed to decipher my own confusion and create an absolutely beautiful cover that conveyed reverse harem and K-Pop. Thank you so much, Natasha!

Then I have a list of amazing beta readers. Brittany, Elizabeth, MiKayla, Megan, Vanessa, Amber, Courtney, Camilla, Nichole, Denise, Melinda, Olivia, Heather, Jessica, Brandie, and Danielle. You guys rock! Sending this out into the world was very nerve-wracking and you all made me feel a lot more reassured about what I was doing. I mean, boy, do I love you guys. I used to think that I was a fast reader. Turns out I'm not. Y'all are so quick to read and you give me such brilliant feedback! Not only did you manage to catch so many typos (I promise it got sent to an editor and proofreader!) but you helped me to develop some of the scenes and characters. Thank you very, very much! Thank you for making Idol Thoughts as good as it is!

ATLANTIS ENTERTAINMENT NEWSLETTER

Would you like to be kept up to date on the antics of the idols and artists at Atlantis Entertainment? Sign up to the Atlantis Entertainment Newsletter, managed by the silent Chairwoman of Atlantis Entertainment, Ji Soo.

Ji Soo will keep you updated on the Atlantis Roster, as well as providing you with a healthy dose of K-Pop, some Korean culture, and if she can persuade her 할머니 (that's Korean for 'grandmother', pronounced halmeoni) to part with some cherished recipes, some of those, along with some reading recommendations. There may even be a few insights into her crazy life. But probably not, because her life is very boring …

Find out more at:

https://sendfox.com/JSLee

ABOUT THE AUTHOR

International Bestselling author, Ji Soo Lee spends most of her days lost in a K-Pop haze, which inspired her to start writing stories about her idols at Atlantis Entertainment.

Under the name Ji Soo Lee, you will find YA contemporary romances, with romance levels like a K-Drama.

Under J. S. Lee, Ji Soo writes steamier stories, mainly of Reverse Harems

WAYS TO CONNECT

Facebook
Author Page:
https://www.facebook.com/OfficialJiSooLee
Atlantis Fan Group:
https://www.facebook.com/groups/AtlantisEnts/

Bookbub:
https://www.bookbub.com/authors/j-s-lee

Amazon:
https://www.amazon.com/J.-S.-Lee/e/B07H353S3L

Instagram:
https://www.instagram.com/ji_soo_lee_author/

Website:
www.jisooleeauthor.com

Pinterest:
https://www.pinterest.com/jisooleeauthor/

Made in the USA
Las Vegas, NV
05 September 2023

77123185R00128